In the Shadow of
the Wonder Wheel

In the Shadow of
the Wonder Wheel

by Carren Strock

© 2012

This is a work of fiction. All the characters and events portrayed in this book
are either fictitious or are used fictitiously.

In-house editor: Ian Randal Strock

Gray Rabbit Publications
1380 East 17 Street, Suite 2233
Brooklyn, New York 11230
www.FantasticBooks.biz

ISBN 10: 1-61720-730-6
ISBN 13: 978-1-61720-730-3

First Edition

This book is dedicated to my incredible family,
who continue to bless me with
their unconditional love and acceptance.

Prologue

Willard Thompson climbed the porch steps and checked the exterior locks on the outside of his front door. He pulled at his boarded-up windows: secure. It didn't hurt to be extra careful. He headed down the alley to the side door, looked around, then turned his key in each of his three locks to let himself into the dark apartment. Quickly he latched the door behind him before turning on the overhead light. The bottle of scotch on the kitchen counter called to him, and he poured a generous amount into a large tumbler. The phone rang. With a deep sigh, he lowered the glass and lifted the receiver.

"Yeah?" he said. He didn't have to look at the caller ID to know who it was. It could only be one of two people calling: the guy who ordered him to do the abortion, or the guy who bought babies.

This was the first. He lifted the notepad and took down the information: obstetrician, location. Then he took down the name, Mallory McGill.

What did the name matter? What did anything matter?

"Are you listening," the voice asked.

"Yeah. I got it," he said.

"She thinks she's having a normal delivery. And oh, she's almost full term."

Those words, "Almost full term," made him smile. A live baby fetched a good bit of change.

Tuesday, July 13
Chapter 1

"Wake up. Wake up, Ms. McGill." Then more loudly, "Ms. McGill, I know you can hear me. I know it."

"Detective, can't you wait with your questions? This girl's lost a lot of blood."

Teri Cardello turned toward the nurse, her eyes still on the girl. "Sorry, nurse. But this girl can hear me. She's not fooling me."

"Teri, let me try." Her partner leaned closer to the bed and said more quietly, "Ms. McGill, I'm Detective Rothman, Sam Rothman. And this is my partner, Teri Cardello. We're here to help you. Can you hear me?"

The young woman raised her fingers slightly. She opened her eyes and squinted against the morning light that flooded the room. She tried to raise her arm to shield them but couldn't. Agitated, she tried harder to move.

"Honey, stay still," the nurse said, adjusting the intravenous line. "Your arm's pinned down."

The girl turned toward the beeping sounds of the monitor beside the bed. She lifted her head slightly. Her grey eyes darted around the room. Her head fell back to the pillow. "Where am I?"

The nurse gently brushed an unruly tangle of pale yellow hair, matted with dry blood, from Mallory's ashen face.

"You're in the hospital. Coney Island Hospital."

"My baby. She came?"

Cardello moved closer. "A better question," she said, doing little to hide the loathing in her voice, "is what did you do with it?"

"What do you mean? What are you talking about?"

"Your baby."

Mallory's eyes opened wide. Her hands shot to her stomach, wrenching the line from her arm. Blood spurted where the needle had been.

"My baby. Where is my baby?" She thrashed about trying to free herself from the bedding tucked around her. Her arms ripped at the sheets that held her.

"Easy honey. Easy. We'll find your baby," the nurse said, pinning her patient's shoulders down.

Mallory wrestled with the sheets. "Please. Please."

The nurse reinserted the IV and taped the needle firmly in place. She adjusted the pressure on the tubing, and the glucose, saline, and antibiotic solutions dripped slowly into the line, through the needle, and into the arm of the terrified girl.

"Can't you see you're upsetting this young woman?"

"It can't be helped. The baby," Cardello demanded moving toward the bed again. "What did you do with your baby?"

The nurse stepped aside.

Rothman moved closer to Cardello. "Ms. McGill," he said more gently, "if there's anything you can tell us. Anything at all…"

"It will go much easier for you if you tell us everything," Cardello interrupted. "Believe me."

The young woman eyed one detective and then the other.

"Teri, give her a chance." Rothman said.

Cardello turned away. She grabbed a pair of rubber gloves from the box on the night stand, slid her hands into them, and opened the locker at the foot of the bed. She stuffed Mallory's brightly colored dress and her white bra into a brown paper bag. Then she put each of her sandals into separate bags.

"What are you doing? I don't understand."

"Evidence. We have to take your things," Rothman said softly.

"Evidence? For what? What happened?" Mallory thrashed about. "I just want my baby."

"I'll bet," Cardello said under her breath.

The physician arrived just then. He looked from the detectives to the distraught woman flailing about in the rumpled bed. "Nurse, get me five milligrams of Valium. Fast."

"Doctor, we need to find that baby."

"Look, I don't know about the baby. This girl was brought to the ER early this morning, hemorrhaging from the vaginal area. We removed her placenta, and stitched up her cervix. She's stabilized now."

"Anything else?"

"A couple of bruises on her buttocks."

"Any foreign substances?"

"No sign of drugs in her toxicology report."

Detective Rothman turned his attention back to Mallory. "Ms. McGill, you have to help us. Your baby may still be alive."

Cardello slammed the locker door shut and, evidence bags in hand, stomped out of the room.

She was at the elevator, banging the button over and over, when Rothman caught up to her. He placed his hand over hers. "That won't make it come any faster, Teri."

The color climbed up and over her high cheekbones as her fury grew. Her olive skin turned crimson. "Maybe it's still alive?" she shrieked.

A passing orderly slowed to see what the commotion was about. Cardello lowered her voice. "Alive? You've got to be kidding. She threw that baby into the creek as sure as, as sure as…. I had to get out of there. Couldn't stand looking at her. Her act didn't fool me."

It was Cardello who usually said, "Let's wait until the evidence is in," but ten years working with her had taught Rothman that nothing made her angrier than a child being victimized, and when it was an infant… well, her rage had to come out. Until she cooled down, and her rational judgment kicked in, trying to reason with her would be useless.

Still, he said quietly, "You've got to stop taking cases like this so personally."

"How should I take it? Honest, decent women try every method known to have a child; adoption, in vitro fertilization, they go through every cent they have, and this—this piece of work—throws her baby into the creek?"

"We don't know that for sure. Maybe something happened—against her will."

"Give me a break, Sam. If you're referring to the case of the baby cut from a pregnant woman's uterus by some nut job, this one's nothing like that. This woman had a vaginal birth."

The shades were closed when Mallory woke again later in the day. A broad-shouldered man sat in the shadows beside the bed.

"Keith, Keith, you're here."

"No, Mallory. It's Brad. Keith's gone. Remember?"

"Oh yes, Keith's gone… but my baby. Brad, where is she?"

Brad reached for Mallory's hand.

"I think you need to tell us that." Detective Cardello said.

Brad and Mallory turned their heads to see two figures standing in the hallway.

"Are you Brad Dawson?"

Brad nodded.

"We found your card in Ms. McGill's pocket."

"Thank you for calling me."

"Would you mind stepping into the hall for a minute?"

Brad turned back to Mallory, smiled, and patted her hand reassuringly. "I'll be right back," he whispered.

"Exactly what is your relationship with Ms. McGill?"

"Why do you want to know that?"

"Your relationship?"

"She was my brother's girlfriend. She was pregnant with his baby."

"Was pregnant?"

"Well, isn't that why she's here—in the maternity ward? She must have had the baby." Dawson caught the glance the two detectives exchanged. "Just what's going on," he asked.

"We'll be asking the questions," Detective Cardello said. "She has the right to a legal defense."

"I'm her legal defense."

And you are…?"

"An attorney."

"How very convenient that she had your card with her."

"I told you, she was my brother's girlfriend. Now you tell me what's going on."

"The police found Ms. McGill near Coney Island Creek. Passed out. Blood all around—on her hands. No sign of the baby. No one else around."

"Oh my god." Brad reached for the wall to support himself. "No. That can't be. It doesn't make any sense."

"A bloody trail to the water… That's all they found. They're preparing to send divers down at dawn."

Brad returned to Mallory's room and pulled the chair closer to the bed. "Mallory," he said taking her hand in his, "you need to tell me what happened."

"Brad, I don't *know* what happened."

"What do you remember? Did you do something?"

"Do what?"

His voice caught, "Kill your baby?"

"Brad, you can't believe that I…"

"Mallory, you know I'm here for you. I'll help you in any way I can, but the evidence… it will be easier if you tell them what happened before they find… the baby's body."

"I don't know. I can't remember anything. Just pain. But my baby—" a look of terror spread across her face, "—she can't be dead."

Brad took her hand in his just as Detective Cardello came into the room. "Don't say anything more now," he whispered.

"Ms. McGill, make sure that you remain in the area. We'll want to talk to you again after the divers finish their search. Is that clear?"

Mallory turned her head away.

"Ms. McGill?"

"I'll take responsibility for Ms. McGill. She'll come home with me," Brad said.

"No. I have to find my baby." Mallory pulled her hand free of Brad's. She shook the bed railing. "Let me out of here. I can't stay here. My baby needs me."

The nurse came in. "Here, here honey. This will relax you."

"No. No. Don't…"

Wednesday, July 14
Chapter 2

Detective Sam Rothman followed a daily routine, and stopping by Rachel's Sweet Shoppe on his way to the 60th Precinct was a vital part of it. This little shop on Neptune Avenue remained a constant in the changing area. Although few tourists ventured into the neighborhood, a mere two blocks inland from the ocean, and the famous Coney Island Boardwalk, the place was a hangout for the local kids.

The cop was a familiar figure, and the kids' loud banter continued undisturbed as the big man made his way through the throng and into the store. He studied the pastries in the glass-covered cake stand. Before he could make a decision, Rachel, the short, round woman behind the crowded counter, wiped her hand on her flowered apron, lifted the cover, and reached in. She pulled out a blueberry muffin, put it on a plate, and laid the plate down in front of him. "Sam, you've been coming here every day for the past ten years. On Wednesday you eat blueberry."

"Come on Rachel, I'm not that predictable."

"Oh yeah?" Rachel ticked off on her fingers, "Wednesday, blueberry muffin, Thursday, Boston creme, Friday, cheese cake, strawberries on top, Saturday, seven layer, Sunday, apple pie, vanilla ice cream on the side…"

"Okay, okay. Maybe I am in some kind of rut."

"What gives? A nice guy like you, you're not half bad looking." She pushed his sandy colored mane out of his eyes. "Maybe a hair cut, a spiffy new shirt. Why don't you give some nice girl a chance?"

"If I could find someone who cooked like you, and looked like you."

"And is a third of my age and half my weight… Yeah, yeah. Don't give me all your bull, Samuel Rothman." Rachel shooed Boots off the stool and plopped her wide bottom down next to Rothman.

"Rachel, I keep telling you, it's against the health laws to keep a cat in a luncheonette. You're going to get into trouble."

She looked around. "What cat? I don't see any cat." Boots, purring, curled his tail around Rothman's leg. "Seriously, Sam," she said in a voice turned maternal. "Isn't it time you settled down with a wife and had yourself a couple of nice kids? I know that's what your mother, may she rest in peace, would have wanted for you."

"Rachel, I'm thirty-eight years old."

"It's never too late."

Rothman ran his hand through his unkempt hair. He'd forgotten to go to the barber again. "I deal with the dregs of the earth. By the time I leave the precinct, I'm not fit company for anyone."

Rachel was instantly on her feet, looking past Rothman toward the open door. "John Kotowsky, you give that to me right now." The boy, shamefaced, handed Rachel the candy bar he'd slipped into his pocket, lowered his head, and turned to leave. "Hey, wait a minute," Rachel stopped the child. Turning him to face her, she lifted his chin. "I just realized, you won the prize."

A big grin crossed the freckled face. "I did?"

"You're the fiftieth person to enter this store today." She handed him a small paper bag. "You get to pick five candy bars."

Elated, the child left the store with his candy.

"Sucker," Rothman said. "You keep making excuses for these little thieves, and I'll be dealing with them in another few years."

Rachel shrugged. "Give the kid a break. The family's on welfare. Four little brothers. The mother's pregnant. Besides, you grew up in those projects, and you didn't turn out so bad yourself."

Rothman bit into the blueberry muffin in front of him.

"So, I heard they found a young girl at the creek Monday night. A self-abortion, botched, or something like that?"

"You're a wonder Rachel. What else have you heard?"

"I'll fill you in when I get the complete scoop. That creek is a cesspool of a place, though, a dumping ground for bodies. Remember that mass-murderer in the nineties? No girl would go there herself, even for an abortion. Doesn't sound right to me." Rachel put two cream-filled doughnuts into a bag. "Say hello to that nice Detective Cardello for me, and give her a treat."

Chapter 3

Mallory heard chatter at the nurses' station outside her room. She heard a cart squeak as it was wheeled down the hall. "Good morning, dearie," a nurse, different than the one she had seen before, opened the blinds. "It's time you were getting up. Isn't it a lovely day?" She cranked the bed until Mallory was sitting, propped against a pillow, her head groggy.

"How long have I been here?"

"Let's see," the nurse took the clipboard from the foot of Mallory's bed and lifted the page. "According to your chart, you lost a great deal of blood and… you were delirious. Pulling out your lines."

"How long have I been here? Tell me." Mallory commanded.

"You were brought in Monday night, and it's Wednesday now."

"Wednesday? Two days. I've got to get out. I've got to find my baby."

"Yes dearie. Of course you do. I'm going to remove your IV now."

As the nurse slowly pulled on one rubber glove and then picked up the other, Mallory ripped the tape and the needle from her arm. "I can't wait."

The nurse stuck a band-aid on the spot Mallory had yanked the needle from, and scooted out of the room just as an aide came in carrying a breakfast tray. The aide put the tray on the table, and positioned it over Mallory's legs. "I'm Delores. You just ring this here buzzer if you want anything more, miss," she said, clipping the control closer to the pillow.

Mallory shoved the tray away. "I've got to get out of here now."

"The doctor will be in with your release papers soon. You can't leave until then."

Mallory fell back to her pillow. She touched her hair, stiff from the dried blood. "Then let me wash."

The aide took a basin and a bar of soap from the night stand beside the bed.

"No. I need to shower."

"Well, all right then." Delores lowered the bed rail and helped Mallory to a sitting position. "You just let your legs dangle over the side of the bed while I adjust the water."

Unsteady, Mallory allowed the aide to help her into the adjoining bathroom. She untied Mallory's cotton gown from behind and slid it forward off her arms. Mallory stepped into the shower and began to pull the plastic curtain closed. The aide held it open. "Rules," she said, "In case you get dizzy or something."

Mallory turned toward the wall. She soaped up her hair, then bent her head slightly to rinse it out. Warm water ran through it, over her milk-laden breasts, and around her stomach, distended from her pregnancy. It mixed with the blood running slowly from between her inner thighs, turning the water a deep pink. A small whirlpool formed and disappeared down the drain. The room began to spin. Mallory grabbed for the shower bar. Delores grabbed her and helped her out of the shower and onto the toilet. She handed Mallory a package of menstrual napkins. Leaning against the sink for support, Mallory did what she needed to do.

The aide then helped her into a clean, faded hospital gown, and led her back to a chair. Quickly she made the bed and Mallory, exhausted, slid between the fresh bed linen.

"So, miss, what time will your husband be coming for you," Delores asked cheerfully.

"My husband? No… He's… he's…" The word *dead* stuck in her mouth.

"Oh you poor thing. I'm so sorry." She patted Mallory's arm. "Well then, I'm sure your family will be coming for you and your baby. They'll take care of you, honey."

Mallory, fighting tears, shook her head slowly.

The woman didn't know what to say. She gathered the dirty bed linen and towels and made a fast exit, nearly bumping into Brad at the doorway.

"Good morning, Mallory," Brad said, "How are you feeling?"

"How should I be feeling? You tell me."

"I uh, I just spoke to the resident. He said you saw the obstetrician."

In listless resignation, Mallory nodded. "He signed my release."

"Well then, I'm going to take you home now. Mrs. Rollins will see to you."

Mallory's head shot up. "No. Not without my baby. What about *her*?"

Brad shrugged. "I don't know." He straddled the straight-backed chair, resting his arms on the back of it. *Just like Keith,* Mallory thought. Keith sat the same way as his brother. The pain of Keith's loss washed over her anew.

"I don't know. I just don't know." Brad, for the first time in his life, was at a loss for words. He lowered his chin to his hands. Normally, he carried himself like a general. Tall, erect. He was a take-charge kind of guy. But today his shoulders slouched as he looked at her. "I don't know what to believe. Get dressed—please, we'll talk more at home."

There was nothing in the crisp voice to remind Mallory of the kind man who had been her good friend these last few months… after Keith's death. Nothing to remind her of the man who'd gone through the Lamaze classes with her and learned the breathing techniques with her. Brad had reassured her that he would be with her for the baby's arrival. But he hadn't been. And where was the baby?

"Get dressed. Please," he said again.

"My clothes?"

Brad opened the locker. It was empty. "Where are the things you were wearing when…"

"The detectives took them."

He walked out to the nurses' station and returned with a hospital gown and a pair of blue paper slippers. He handed them to her, then pulled the curtain around the bed.

"It wasn't supposed to be like this—none of it was. Something went terribly wrong," Mallory sobbed.

"I know. Please, get dressed. We'll sort this all out."

"Sort this all out? We're not talking about a pile of laundry. My *baby* is missing.

"Mallory, calm yourself. Be glad they're allowing you to come home with me, and not taking you into custody."

The hospital gown she wore opened in the back. Mallory pulled the second one over the first so that it opened in the front. She slid her feet into the slippers. She didn't ask about the overnight bag that had stood ready in her foyer, carefully packed for her return home. Brad knew about it, but he hadn't brought it. Maybe because it had clothing for the baby's trip home, too; the little white onesie with the tiny pink flower appliques she'd stitched around the neck, and the small pink sweater and hat she'd knitted when she'd been told she was going to have a little girl.

"I'm ready."

Brad pulled back the curtain. She reached for his hand.

Delores came in with a wheelchair. "I'm so sorry, miss. They told me…"

"I don't want that," Mallory said, ignoring the aide's offer of sympathy.

"Hospital rules," she said apologetically.

"But…" Mallory began.

The aide looked to Brad for help.

"Mal, please," he said.

Mallory slumped into the wheelchair.

"I'm going for the car. I'll meet you out front." He patted her shoulder, one pat, and left.

Delores put a blanket over Mallory's lap and pushed the chair down the long hall, past rooms with smiling people, flowers, and happy chatter. Then they passed the nursery and heard babies crying.

"Wait." Mallory leaned to her right and grabbed the frame of the large viewing window. The wheelchair stopped short. She placed her hands on the window and studied the row after row of clear plastic bassinets. The babies were swaddled in pink and blue striped blankets, and each wore a tiny knitted cap."

"Miss, she's not there," the aide said gently, taking Mallory's hands from the glass and putting them in her lap. They entered the elevator and rode down in silence.

Once outside the hospital, Delores pushed her chair beside the driveway to wait for Brad. She angled it away, but Mallory had already seen the wheelchair beside hers, with the woman cradling a sleeping infant in her arms. She'd seen the older woman beaming with pride and holding a vase filled with small pink carnations and baby's breath flowers. She'd seen the helium balloons tied to the vase proclaiming "It's a Boy" as they bobbed in the gentle breeze. And she'd seen a smiling man snapping picture after picture. *A scene from a Norman Rockwell painting,* Mallory thought.

She looked down at her own arms, empty in her lap. She wrapped them tightly around her body, but they couldn't relieve the icy coldness that had settled in her middle.

Brad pulled up to the curb in his BMW, and waited behind the wheel as Delores helped Mallory out of the chair and into the car. When she was settled in, he pulled away from the curb and drove north on Ocean Parkway.

Mallory glanced over at him. He seemed to be collecting his thoughts. "Mallory," he said finally, in his gentlest voice, the one he used when he was interrogating a witness, "some women go off the deep end when they have a baby. Hormones and things change. They do crazy things. They're not responsible. I'll help you. All I need to hear is the truth. Tell me what happened to the baby. The only reason you haven't been indicted is because the police haven't found the body yet."

"Brad, I…" She began and then sighed. What was the truth? She leaned back in the seat and lapsed into silence. All she could think about was her baby. Where was she now? What had happened to her? Why did they think she had killed her? Those detectives. Even Brad. He was angry with her because she couldn't remember. What could she say? She couldn't have done anything so horrible, could she? No. She'd wanted this baby, Keith's baby.

Brad turned right on Avenue M, and continued on to Bedford Avenue, where he turned left. Only his fingers drumming on the steering wheel broke the silence of the drive.

They'd said her hands were red with blood. She lifted them now and turned them over. Her palms were blue, cobalt blue. She was still looking at them when Brad pulled into the driveway. He drove alongside the manicured lawn, bordered with clusters of impatiens and coleus, to the right side of the large house, and stopped the car. He came around and opened her door.

Dizzy, Mallory leaned against the car. She looked up at the stately home she'd always loved—not because of its size, or its gracious veranda, but because Keith had grown up here, raised by his grandfather. Each time she visited she had fantasized about how they would come to visit with their babies and how happy the old gentleman would be to watch little ones playing in his lovely yard.

Suddenly, it all came rushing back to her. Keith was gone, that terrible accident. His grandfather dead several days later—from the shock of losing his grandson, people said. And now her baby was gone. She collapsed, sliding to the ground clasping her stomach and sobbing.

Mrs. Rollins came running from the kitchen door. "There, there, child. It will be all right." She pushed Brad away from the car and knelt beside Mallory. With the corner of her starched white apron, she wiped Mallory's tear-stained face. Then, she put her arms around the shivering girl. "Up with you. Gently now." Tall, and deceptively strong for an old woman, she had no trouble getting Mallory to her feet.

Brad, standing off to the side, looked at Mallory sadly. Mrs. Rollins wrapped her arms more protectively around the girl and urged her past him, but Mallory stopped.

"Brad," she looked into his eyes. "How could you even think I could do such an awful thing."

He turned his gaze from her. "Tell me then, where is my brother's baby?"

Mallory had no answer.

Mrs. Rollins half led, half carried her into the house, up the wide carpeted stairway, and down the hall into the large corner bedroom. Mallory held the post of the great canopy bed while the housekeeper pulled back the comforter and fluffed the pillows. She sat Mallory down on the bed, slipped off the hospital gowns.

"Mrs. Rollins, I have to find my baby."

"I know. I know. You'll find her after you nap. Everything will come clear then." She slipped one of her own cotton nightgowns over Mallory's head. "Here, this will help you to rest." She pulled a pill bottle from her apron pocket and gave a tablet to Mallory, along with a glass of water she poured from the bedside decanter.

The bedroom was pitch dark when Mallory awoke.

"No," she cried out, memories of a cold black cellar, crawly things, vivid in her mind's eye. "Not the dark. No. Please." As a foster child, she'd been locked in that cellar each time she wet her pants, and she'd never overcome her fear of the dark.

Groggy, she fumbled for the bedside lamp. It crashed to the floor.

Mrs. Rollins opened the door, the light from the hallway breaking the darkness. "There, there child. You were having a nightmare. You're all right now."

"All right?" Her hands went to her empty stomach. "How could I be all right?"

"I know dear, I didn't mean…" She sat on the edge of the bed and rubbed Mallory's back.

Mallory's tight muscles slowly relaxed. The softness of the feather pillow drew her in, but she refused to close her eyes.

"Here you go, take this," Mrs. Rollins reached into her pocket and opened the bottle of pills. "This will help you to relax."

"I don't want to relax."

"You have to take this. It's Mr. B's orders." She filled a glass with water from the decanter that had been spared when the lamp fell over.

"All right. If Brad says to." Mallory swallowed the pill. "Maybe a little rest. Yes. After I rest. I'll find her then."

Chapter 4

Willard Thompson pulled up to the broken curb. He gazed up at the three-story frame house he'd purchased the year before, the last in a row of four attached dwellings. Peeling paint, warped boards, rot, decay. A drug addict tenant on the top floor. This house was just what he wanted. He'd already done his homework.

When city projects went up in the '70s, Coney Island's middle class, with its small mom-and-pop businesses, fled to the suburbs. For a while, a sense of community had continued to exist because the projects were few in number, but when the Housing Authority razed entire neighborhoods and replaced them with dozens of additional 18-24 story public housing projects, the area was thrown out of balance. Thompson's street was one of the last remaining that hadn't been taken over by these projects yet.

The remaining few houses on the block, including his, were slated for demolition in another year or so. He planned to be out before then.

A narrow alley led to a side door near the rear of his house. He could bring in the equipment necessary for his plans. No one would ask questions in this area, a dumping ground for the old, the poor, and the misplaced. He could live here, do what he wanted to, and come and go without raising suspicion.

Things had gone well. He'd taken care of enough women to pad his suitcase in preparation for his escape to freedom. Now, all he needed were two more deals, and he would be out of here.

He'd gone out earlier than usual for his groceries. In another hour, parking would be impossible in this neighborhood. The streets would be mobbed with summer crowds heading to the beaches just a couple of blocks away.

The sea air was warm and the day sunny, but a chill coursed through his body. He never got used to the dirty work he did.

Shoulders hunched, and groceries in one arm, he walked slowly down the narrow alley, toward the rear of the dilapidated building. As he walked, he ran his fingers tentatively along the rusted storm fence. It had become one with a spindly hedge that separated the right side of his property from a trash-filled lot.

Thompson reached down and scooped up a handful of dry, sandy dirt from his weed infested yard. His thin lips tightened. This was a far cry from the neat little cape he and Abby, his wife, had lived in. White, with black shutters. Potted pink geraniums on the sides of the front steps. He thought about his lilac bushes and the flower gardens he'd cultivated—the most beautiful on the street. He thought about the way he had methodically planned his life. If only he'd listened to his wife.

Twenty years had passed, and that last scenario still played over and over in his head.

From the first time Abby had met Manny she'd said, "That Manny gives me the creeps. Keep your distance from him. I have a bad feeling."

But Thompson always defended his friend. "Manny was always there for me," he'd tell her. "Even when he flunked out of the university, and I went on to medical school. And when I began my practice, he sent patients my way."

Then, one evening, while Thompson and Abby were playing with little Isabell, the phone rang. It was Manny.

"Willard, you've got to help me out. I got this good Catholic girl knocked up. She has some sort of medical condition, and should never have got herself pregnant."

"Abortions are legal now," Thompson said. "I'll give you the number of a clinic."

"I can't. She's in her third trimester."

"Christ."

"Her priest told her if she died having the baby, it would be God's will, and she should accept that. By the time she decided not to listen to him, she was too far along for a legal abortion. You've got to help me. I'll be in big trouble if you don't."

"No, Manny, I won't."

Manny was loud, and Abby overheard the phone conversation. She gathered Isabell in her arms. "If you do, we won't be here when you get back."

Thompson had laughed. "Don't be ridiculous. Making that girl carry to term even though it would kill her? How ethical would that be? Besides, he's my friend. And he's always been so generous."

"This is what I think of his generosity," Abby picked up Thompson's cherished porcelain vase—Manny's wedding gift to them—and she flung it against the fireplace marble.

It should have been a simple procedure—he hadn't expected those complications. Unfortunately, something went wrong and the girl lay dying in his office.

"I have friends," Manny said. "We'll get rid of her body."

But the strong ethics of the young medical doctor would not allow him to do that. He knew he had done wrong. But he tried to right it—to save the girl. He called for an ambulance—a decision that cost him dearly.

True to her word, his wife and the baby he adored were gone when he returned home from jail several days later.

Manny had cut out before the ambulance arrived. Thompson surrendered his passport and had all of his assets liquidated to post the high bail—for each alleged murder, and then he faced the trial alone.

He'd had no contact, no word from his wife, all these years. All of this was his reward for helping a friend.

Embittered, the young doctor turned to whiskey. "The only career I ever wanted, the only woman I ever loved, my precious child lost to me forever." He mumbled to anyone who would listen. "It was the system. The system destroyed me."

His thick dark hair fell out. His teeth rotted. In three years, he had become one with the cesspool of humanity that lay on the streets of the Bowery. The few little patches of now-grey hair that remained, hung over his shoulders, matted with filth. Deep furrows creased his forehead and ran through his stubble, down the rough sides of his pitted red nose to the edges of his down-turned lips.

Manny found Willard Thompson slumped against a cracked wall, a bottle of cheap wine in one hand and the handle of a tattered doctor's bag grasped firmly in the other. Thompson had always been so proud of that bag, his first purchase when he graduated from medical school. Manny recognized the broken man by the worn leather bag, and by his signature, coke-bottle glasses, now held together with twine and gobs of masking tape.

"I was a doctor. A fine doctor. The only career I ever wanted…"

"Willard, it's me, Manny."

"…the only woman I ever loved, my precious child lost to me forever," he mumbled, grabbing Manny's lapel.

Manny, choking on the foul odor of decay that came from Thompson's mouth, turned his face away. "Pull yourself together, man."

Thompson pulled Manny closer.

Manny shoved him away, and straightened the lapel of his expensive suit. "You smell like a filthy, stinking urinal."

Thompson crumpled to the street, his face inches away from the gutter.

When Manny returned a short time later with a cup of black coffee from the food cart vendor on the corner, Thompson was sitting against a fire hydrant, cheap wine running from his mouth.

"Drink this, then we'll talk," Manny said, pulling the bottle from Thompson's filthy hand and replacing it with a Styrofoam coffee cup.

"Leave me alone," Thompson said, his words slurring and his coffee spilling. His leg jerked as the hot liquid soaked through his pants, but he didn't notice. "Just give me my bottle."

"Listen to me." Manny took off his own jacket and, using the sleeves as gloves to avoid any bodily contact, shook Thompson until he seemed to focus. "I've been looking for you for the past two years. My connections—the syndicate, uh, I mean my silent partners, they need the talents of a doctor."

"A doctor? I was a doctor. A fine doctor. The only career I ever wanted…"

Manny shook him again until he seemed to focus. "You have a choice. You can stay in the gutter, or work again… for me.

"Work? Practice medicine?" The broken man's hands began to shake. He clutched his bag tightly to him. "Anything. I'll do anything you want."

It took several months for Manny to get Thompson cleaned up and sober. With proper diet, his gaunt frame filled out. His hair began to grow back. New glasses replaced his broken, taped-together ones. Manny gave him a fictitious name and false identification, and set him up in an elegant limestone townhouse, across the street from New York City's Central Park. In return, Thompson tended gun shots and other wounds inflicted during illegal skirmishes between the unscrupulous. He also performed abortions on their women—whether the women wanted them or not.

Manny paid all of the expenses. He gave Thompson no cash. Thompson was dependent on Manny for everything; from the toilet paper he used to the coffee he drank, to the daily newspapers he read. But Manny also secured whatever drugs Thompson needed for his practice—no questions asked. And Thompson had been ordering extra and stashing the excess away. Drugs could always be sold—once he found a contact.

After he'd lost Manny's pregnant friend, and while he awaited the outcome of his trial, Willard Thompson read everything he could about late-term abortions. Although once the results of the trial came in— acquitted of premeditated murder, medical license revoked—it didn't matter, until Manny pulled him out of the gutter and set him up in the Manhattan town house.

The first time a woman in her third trimester was brought to him for an abortion, he panicked. Then, as he began to work on her, the information he'd absorbed through his studies came rushing back to him. There were no complications for the woman, and he delivered a viable baby—dead.

For the first few years, no amount of washing had made him feel clean. And then the time came when he no longer felt anything—until he read about Dantano, a man accused of being a baby broker. That was when he realized there was a way he could save himself. He followed the case closely. Dantano walked free after a long trial, not because he was found innocent, but because the key witness mysteriously disappeared. Rather than abort the late-term fetuses, Thompson could salvage them, and sell them—to this Dantano.

Not many viable fetuses came his way, but when they did, they paid well… and in cash. Willard Thompson stashed his money away—not sure just how he'd get out of the business, or how much money would be enough to do so, until he saw a documentary on Alaska. He fell in love with its wide expanse and isolation.

That following December, Thompson asked Manny for some cash, telling him he wanted to go to Miami for a couple of weeks to get the chill out of his bones. Instead, he'd gone to Alaska and bought two acres of land, about an hour outside of Anchorage. He'd paid twenty grand. When he returned, he told Manny how much he had loved the South and the warm climate, so Manny would think he'd head there when he ran off.

Just another thirty thousand and he could build a small log cabin. He counted his money. Almost enough. He didn't keep it in a bank, and he had no credit cards. There would be no paper trail for the syndicate or Dantano to trace back to him.

He was so close to his goal. Then a neighbor got curious. Thompson saw her looking in his window and then snooping through his garbage after he'd performed an abortion. No. He couldn't let anything stop him now.

He pulled up the floorboard in the space he'd hollowed out under his kitchen cabinet, and grabbed his old medical bag with the false bottom a shoemaker had sewn in for him. That false bottom held his phony passports and all of his money. He also grabbed the small suitcase in which he'd been stashing the extra drugs, and ran out the door.

He caught the first subway, the number 4. At Atlantic Avenue it was held up for track work, so he changed to the first train that came, the Q train. The next thing he knew he was in Coney Island, holed up in a cheap rooming house near the train terminal.

Thompson's dreary room—with its peeling grey wallpaper, narrow cot, bureau missing a drawer, and lone lightbulb dangling from the ceiling —was a far cry from the townhouse Manny had set him up in. It was no bigger than his prison cell had been, but here he had a door that he could open and close, and lock or unlock, when *he* wanted to.

This seedy part of Coney Island was a far cry from the magical place he remembered as a youth. Although the Wonder Wheel still turned, used furniture storefronts had taken over the north side of Surf Avenue where majestic horses had once whirled around on the carousel. He remembered his father holding him as he leaned over to grab the gold ring.

The carousel was now dismantled and packed away to become a landmark on the boardwalk someday. The independent owners and vendors were gone, too. Luna Park had reopened, on the shuttered

Astroland site. The Scream Zone, featuring two major roller coasters, had opened, and in the new Steeplechase Coaster, riders sat on racehorse seats resembling Coney Island's classic Steeplechase ride.

Along the boardwalk, a feeling of decay blended with a palpable sense of Americana where the neon signs at Nathan's and the Cyclone fairly oozed nostalgia. But none of this interested Thompson.

He was busy getting a new set of papers and changing his appearance. His hair had grown back, but he shaved his head. His beard grew in white, with some peppery grey sprinkled in. And he underwent laser eye surgery —something his wife had suggested he do years before. The first time he saw his reflection without his thick glasses, he did a double-take. Even he had trouble recognizing himself, and he was pleased. He spent his time collecting, and then poring over, any bit of information he could gather on Alaska, determined to find a way to get the rest of the money he needed for his escape.

Chapter 5

Mallory lay in the large canopy bed trying to put the pieces together. But what were the pieces? Could she have lost her mind? Why couldn't she remember? "Try Mal, try," she told herself. "What happened? Think girl. Think."

She had read about a Texas woman who had drowned her five children in the bathtub. And there was another woman who had driven her two beautiful little boys into a lake in South Carolina. Was she like those women? Could she have committed such a horrendous crime—throwing her own baby into a creek, that creek? She couldn't imagine herself ever doing something so hideous—but she couldn't be sure.

No. She would never hurt her baby. Never. She wanted this baby. Keith and she had chosen her name together. It was on their first date. They'd gone to the Plaza Hotel's Palm Court for lunch. A large painting of a child hung in the foyer. They'd both been taken by the mischievous grin on the precocious six-year-old called Eloise, who, as the story went, lived in the hotel and ran free getting into all sorts of mischief.

An orphan, Mallory had lived most of her childhood in foster homes, watching life from the periphery. She'd hoped that her Eloise would grow up as happy and carefree as that child from the Plaza.

She turned on her stomach and punched the pillow over and over. "Oh Keith," she sobbed. "Why did you leave me? Why did you have to die? Why? Why? If only you were here, this nightmare never would have happened, and our baby would be here now."

The satin bedding in the elegant room offered her little comfort, and she tossed and turned. Finally, curled up into a tight ball, longing to become a tiny speck and disappear, she fell into a fitful sleep. *Bright, fast-moving lights, a car, a man. Speeding down Ocean Parkway. Going south toward Coney Island Hospital. Soon,* Mallory thought. *Soon I'll have my baby. But the driver kept going. She gasped. A contraction stiffened her body.*

"Turn here. Turn here," she pleaded, clutching her stomach as another contraction wracked her body. He didn't respond. He continued

driving past the hospital. Maybe he hadn't heard. She moved forward and, from the edge of the back seat, reached toward his shoulder. He turned to look at her. Then, turning back to the road, he swerved to avoid an oncoming car. Losing her balance, she reached out to grab the head rest in front of her. She grabbed the driver instead and—and—everything went blank.

Mallory awoke with a start, her body drenched in perspiration. Images of the car and driver stayed with her. Her dream had to be real. She couldn't have made it all up. She had seen him. There had been a driver. But what was it she couldn't remember? What had happened after she'd grabbed him?

"I don't care what happens to me," she said, moving toward the edge of the bed and sliding her feet to the carpeted floor. "But I owe it to you, my little Eloise. I promise I *will* find you."

Mallory sat at the edge of the bed formulating her plan. Even though Brad said she couldn't, and even if she might be violating some stupid rule by leaving his house, she didn't care. She had to go back to her own place for clothes, money, and her car keys, so that she could begin her search.

It took some time before Mallory had the strength to drag herself out of bed and to the bathroom. Mrs. Rollins, always so efficient, had laid out towels, a packaged toothbrush, and a bar of Mallory's favorite scented soap, Lily of the Valley. She'd also remembered a box of maxi pads, and left that on the sink as well.

Mallory brushed her teeth, then splashed water on her face. Had she bothered to look up, the face in the mirror would have shocked her. Her hair, usually falling freely in unruly abandon, hung dry and lusterless, accenting the paleness of her normally flushed cheeks. Only the dark grey shadows under her eyes gave color to her ghostly pallor.

The cool tiled floor reminded Mallory that she had no shoes other than the paper ones from the hospital, and only the hospital gown to cover herself with. She returned to the bedroom and opened the large wardrobe. It was empty. Then she opened each drawer of the bureau. Nothing. Slowly, she opened the door to the hall—just a crack. She could hear Brad on the phone downstairs, although she couldn't make out what he was saying.

She tiptoed to the next door, to the room that had been Keith's. White sheets covered all of his furniture. She moved the sheets aside to search the armoire and the chest of drawers. His clothes were gone.

The next room was the sewing room. This room she knew was Mrs. Rollins' sanctuary, even though her antique treadle sewing machine was now dwarfed by the elaborate Victorian desk that had come, with two chairs, from the old Mr. Dawson's office. The two chairs, covered in a masculine plaid, stood on either side of the draped window. A small table between the chairs held a pile of Mrs. Rollins' two favorite newspapers; the *Daily News* and the *National Enquirer*. A large wardrobe completed the furnishings in the room. Mallory went directly to the wardrobe and opened the doors. A hint of camphor wafted through the air.

The largest shelf held an assortment of elegant frocks in silks and velvets. Another held four flowered hat boxes. And still another shelf held old brittle copies of news clippings. Two large wicker baskets sat on the top-most shelf. She reached up and tilted the first. It tipped over. Old photographs and playbills fell to the floor. She gathered them hurriedly and threw them back into the basket. Then, more carefully, tipped the second container. Old baby clothes. Her heart gave a tug.

She glanced at the painting on the wall beside the door as she made her exit. It was the one of Brad as a small child. She had copied it from an old photograph, not knowing it was Brad at the time.

She hurried to the next door. It had to be Brad's room. Sure enough, on the far wall, a huge wardrobe held his clothes. Mallory tore off Mrs. Rollins' nightgown and pulled on a pair of sweat pants. She grabbed a light blue oxford shirt, pulled it over her head without stopping to unbutton it, grabbed a pair of sneakers, and crept back into the hall.

Brad's muffled conversation came through the office door, slightly ajar to the left of the stairs. Mallory made her way down the carpeted stairs holding the sneakers against her chest. She couldn't chance going past his office to the front door, so she turned right and right again, and padded quietly through the dark hallway beside the stairs, then through the large kitchen and past the pantry. From a door beside it, she heard Mrs. Rollins snoring. Finally, she made her way through the laundry room to the back door. Remembering that there was a night alarm, she hesitated. Had Brad set it yet? Very slowly she inched the door open. The night was bright with stars. No signal sounded. Only after she'd quietly closed the door behind her did she let out her breath and slip on Brad's too-large sneakers.

To get to the street, she would have to walk through the driveway which was brightly lit, but Brad would surely see her from the large window in his study which opened onto the driveway. Then she remembered something Keith had once told her. Hidden by a peony bush, there was an opening in the backyard hedge. He and Brad used to sneak out of the yard through it when they were children. The yard was large, and it was too dark to see the bush, but Mallory took a deep breath. Sure enough, the aroma of the peony—romantic, powdery—led her right to it.

She squeezed behind the bush and passed through the opening into the neighbor's yard.

What little energy she had was fast disappearing. Still, determined, she shuffled along in the oversized sneakers. Once she reached the sidewalk, she made her way along it clinging to the thick hedges or wrought iron fences that fronted most of the mansions. On Avenue M, she stopped at a lamppost to catch her breath. Here the houses grew smaller. Leaning now against the cars parked at the curb as she went, Mallory inched her way along the street.

Blood began to trickle down her thighs. The nurse had warned Mallory of the possibility of hemorrhaging but, determined to get her car keys and begin her search, she had ignored the instructions. Past East 24th, 23rd, 22nd she dragged herself. Blood ran down her legs and seeped into the sneakers, but she paid no attention as she counted down to East 17th Street.

The streets were silent, even across Ocean Avenue where stores, gated for the night, replaced the private homes. She turned onto her street, and then into the courtyard of her apartment building, where she stopped to take another deep breath. Just as she was about to let out a huge sigh, she noticed Mr. Lowenthal sitting at his open window, next to the building's main entrance, and exhaled slowly instead. Not wanting to be drawn into conversation, she stepped out of the sticky sneakers and walked quietly past his window.

The door to the entry hall was unlocked, and someone had wedged the inner door open, so there was no need to ring one of her neighbors' bells to be buzzed in. Mallory hurried to the elevator. A handwritten sign taped to the door read "Elevator out of service." She leaned against the wall to the left and breathed deeply. Then, clutching the handrail, began to climb the stairs, pausing to catch her breath on each landing. On the fifth landing, she lowered herself to the steps and rested for a few minutes. At the head of the stairs, a radiator sat under the hall window that had been covered over with black paint. She slid her hand behind it and found her spare key, on the baseboard molding where she kept it for emergencies.

Her apartment was dark, except for the glow of the night light from the kitchen. But that was all Mallory needed. In the hall closet, on the uppermost shelf, she found her box of kotex. She took an old denim skirt from another shelf and slipped it on. Next, she grabbed a lightweight sweater and her sneakers.

Her hand rested briefly on the closed door beside the hall closet. She shuddered. She wanted to, but couldn't bear to turn the knob. After a few minutes, she pulled herself away and went back to the kitchen. Her watch and favorite bracelet were where she had left them when she'd gone to have her baby. Keith had bought her a beautiful gold bracelet, but she preferred the cheap plastic one he'd won for her the first time they'd gone to Coney Island. She slipped that on. Then she took the money she'd saved from the tea kettle on the shelf, and thrust it into her pocket. Anxious to get to the hospital when she'd gone into labor, she'd forgotten to take her cell phone with her. Now she slipped that into her rear pocket. Then she reached for her car keys on the hook near the door. Just as she was about to leave, the door to the apartment opened. Brad and Mrs. Rollins stood there.

In the past
Chapter 6

The apartments in Thompson's rooming house had been subdivided, and the larger rooms divided yet again into smaller rooms. This hodgepodge of rooms lodged an assortment of characters. There was Simon, a soldier who'd gotten screwed up during the Gulf War and walked around talking to himself. There was also the dwarf who recited Shakespeare, and the old woman Olivia, with the pink rouged cheeks who, in her youth, had been an actress. He knew because, although his room had a sink, the communal toilet was at the end of the hall, past her room, and she kept her door open. So each time he needed to piss, she stopped him to show him the same pictures. There was also the woman with the high-heeled red boots, black fish-net stockings, short slitted black leather skirt, and low-cut red blouse: a hooker, judging by her look and the hours she kept. And last, there was Vickie, the fresh-faced young woman who had almost knocked him over as she ran toward the toilet, a book in hand, and her auburn ponytail bobbing, on his first day there. It was days before he realized that she and the hooker were one and the same.

Passing each other on the stairs, or in the hall, Vickie and Thompson formed a nodding acquaintance, and it was Vickie who gave him the solution to his money problem.

One night, he found her crying in the stairwell. At first he continued up the stairs, on his way up to his room, having sworn to himself that he wouldn't get involved with anyone else's problems ever again. But his old ethics were still with him. He turned back and sat beside her.

"I'm pregnant and I just can't have this baby. I've got to get rid of it."

"How far along are you," Thompson asked.

"Four weeks. I'm very regular and I know when it happened. The bastard refused to use a condom. I turned to leave and he grabbed me and," she shuddered, "… he raped me."

Thompson walked her back to her room. "I'll take care of everything. You don't have to wor…" His words stuck in his throat as he opened her door and stepped into a large, freshly painted, and immaculately clean room. Pale yellow walls set off the bed, tucked in a corner and adorned with yellow flowered sheets, ruffled pillows, and a coordinating spread. Matching ruffled curtains fluttered at the clean window, open to catch the sea air. Two white wicker chairs, and a matching wicker table, faced the window with its flowering plants on the sill. The one lone cooking appliance, a hotplate, sat on the dormitory sized refrigerator in another corner, and beside that, a tin tub for bathing stood upright.

Thompson put a pot of water on her hotplate to boil. "I'll be right back," he assured her, and returned to his room to retrieve his bag from the small closet he'd secured with a padlock.

He prepared his instruments, making certain to boil the syringe an adequate amount of time. A sedative helped Vickie to relax and reduce her cramping as he began the suction-aspiration. Five minutes later she was resting comfortably, the procedure completed.

A few weeks after that, Thompson heard heels clicking on the stairs, then he heard Vickie's door next to his opening. He didn't want to listen, but couldn't help overhearing the conversation.

"Vickie, Vickie, I'm knocked up. I don't want to go back to that clinic. All that paperwork, hours of counseling about my options. I know all that shit. Fuck. Fuck. What am I gonna do?"

Vickie brought her friend to Thompson, and she brought other hooker friends to him. Word spread. Cash abortions, no questions asked. And his business grew. But it was chancy working out of his room, or theirs. He needed more space and the right equipment. That was what brought him to the dilapidated house off Surf Avenue.

The abortions he did now were first or second term—unsalvageable fetuses, at the request of the pregnant women themselves, but this one was different.

Some guy had gotten his number from Vickie. "It's against the woman's wishes," the caller told him, "but there will be a large payment if you keep your mouth shut and do as you're told—no questions asked." At first he refused. Then he looked around his squalid quarters. The money from this one job on a Mallory McGill, and the sale of her viable baby afterward, would give him just the amount he needed to get out of this filthy business for good.

Thompson didn't want to call Dantano. He'd skipped town without leaving a forwarding address, and the baby buyer didn't have a forgiving nature. But Dantano had contacts and big bucks. He sat down on his cot and lifted the phone from the small table beside it. His fingers twitched as he made the call.

Wednesday, July 14
Chapter 7

Brad and Mrs. Rollins escorted Mallory back to Brad's house from her apartment. Then Mrs. Rollins led her upstairs to the corner bedroom. She closed the door and Mallory heard the key click in the lock behind her.

"Mr. B told me to do this—for your own good Ms. McGill."

Mallory sat down on the bed. Even if Brad hadn't found her and brought her back, where would she have gone? Where would she have started her search? She put her head in her hands. Her eye caught the white card between the bed and the chair. "Detective Rothman," it read. What was it he'd said? "If there's anything you think of, anything at all, give me a call." Mallory slipped the card into her pocket.

Exhausted, she lay down and dozed. *Bright lights. Shrieking. Cheering. Laughing. Men yelling. A baby crying.* Mallory gasped. Her eyes opened wide. "My baby is alive. I know it. I know it!"

She pulled herself out of the bed and banged on the door. "Brad, Brad, let me out." After a few minutes of banging, she heard footsteps. Brad opened the door, Mrs. Rollins, at his side. "Calm yourself, Mallory," he said.

"You've got to help me," Mallory pleaded, grabbing Brad. "I have to retrace my steps to see…"

Mrs. Rollins stepped into the room and peeled Mallory's hand from Brad's arm. Firmly, she led the hysterical girl back to the bed. "Breathe girl, breathe."

Mallory sat down and took a deep breath, and then another.

"There now. That's better, isn't it?" Mrs. Rollins asked rubbing her shoulder.

"My baby's alive. I can't remember much about that night she disappeared, but I know she's alive. I just know it."

Brad looked to Mrs. Rollins. The housekeeper shook her head. "Then where is she," she asked gently.

"I don't know but I *feel* it. It's something I just *feel*."

"Brad, please. You have to help me."

"I'd like to, but I just don't know what I can do until you give me more information. I need the facts. I'm sorry Mallory." Brad turned and walked away.

"Miss McGill, Mr. B said if you were in any distress, I was to give you one of these," the housekeeper poured some water from the bedside pitcher. She put her arm around Mallory's shoulders and forced the pill between the girl's clenched lips. Lacking the strength to fight, Mallory took the glass of water and swallowed the pill.

The sound of a crying baby haunted her as she drifted off into another restless sleep.

Chapter 8

Mr. Lowenthal had turned off the flame. The whistling kettle ceased its whistle. He held his finger on the rim of the cup as he poured the boiling water. With precise steps, he walked to the counter and reached for the tea box. Three quick whiffs and he had the one he wanted, the camomile tea. Yup. He did just fine for himself. "Edith, see that? You needn't have worried," he said to her presence, still in the room after eighteen years.

The night had smelled of dust, dryness. The air carried a chill. Mr. Lowenthal, tea in hand, was settled into the large wing backed chair at the front window when he heard the footsteps tiptoe across the courtyard. The light scent of lily of the valley drifted through the window. "Sure is a pretty evening, isn't it Ms. McGill," he would have said if the young woman had stopped to chat, but Mr. Lowenthal sensed an urgency in her step, a preoccupation with something, and didn't impose. Eight pages of Braille later, other footsteps entered the building, and six pages after that, Ms. McGill left with those footsteps. One set belonged to Brad Dawson, Keith's brother. He knew him by his aftershave lotion. He'd bet the bank it was him, but the other set he couldn't place.

A short time later, Mr. Lowenthal heard the thud, thud, thud of a basketball. "Hey Moses, how's it going?"

"Damn, Mr. L. You always know it's me. Even in the dark."

Mr. Lowenthal chuckled. "Up to no good, I presume?"

"Why you always presume that?"

"Maybe because it's past midnight, and you live way over in Coney Island."

"Yeah, yeah. Had some business out this way. You know how it is." The thudding receded as the teenager moved away from the window and toward the front door in the courtyard.

"Ms. McGill's not home."

The thudding stopped. "Thanks, Mr. L. Later." The thudding resumed, growing louder as he passed the window, and then receding once again as he headed down the street.

"Edith," Mr. Lowenthal said to his deceased wife, "you never know. A weird combination they make. Mallory McGill, 28 years old with a degree in design from Parsons, and Moses, an 18-year-old with a degree in life from the school of hard knocks. Always seems to have a strong sense of right and wrong, that boy. Highly respected on the street, I hear. His friends call him the Judge.

"Sometimes I can't tell who's mentoring who."

Mallory had introduced Moses to Mr. Lowenthal when he'd first started coming around to her place two months earlier. She'd been volunteering at a youth center, teaching little ones to paint, and had been asked to paint a mural on the building. The committee had left the subject matter up to her and, in an attempt to discourage the graffiti artists from reclaiming the wall, Mallory had decided to paint something they could identify with. She designed a montage superimposing depictions of the local kids playing sports, and she'd described it to Mr. Lowenthal in such vivid detail that the blind man could almost feel the wash of blue/grey, then, the deeper hues. And he could almost see the movement of the piece.

But as the days passed, she became more and more discouraged.

"Each morning, I return to find my work defaced with graffiti," she had told him. "I remove the offensive words and gang logos and continue with my painting, and each evening, the neighborhood vandals return to deface my work again."

Then, one day, Lowenthal heard Mallory getting out of her car and singing as she came toward the building. He chanted, "*Ma nishtanah halailah hazeh mikol halaylot,*" taking the Hebrew words "Why is this night different from all other nights of the year," from the four questions recited at Passover.

She laughed. "Moses is the answer."

"So you know the Passover story?" Lowenthal had said.

"No. Moses is *my* answer. I was doing quick studies of the kids at recess—for my mural. In an instant I was surrounded by a bunch of teens on bikes and skateboards. One boy grabbed my art box and tossed it to another. A girl grabbed my sketch pad and began ripping out the pages. The kids were playing their own version of 'monkey in the middle'—and I was the monkey. Then, this Moses arrived with a basketball under his arm and instantly, all of the kids stopped what they were doing. He clicked his fingers and reached out his hand. The girl with my drawings handed them to him. All of the art supplies that had been thrown around the street were laid at my feet.

"I started to thank him," Mallory told Mr. Lowenthal. "Moses said, 'messing with folks—get you into big trouble.'"

"I was only sketching," I said.

"You was encroaching on peoples' territory."

"Mr. Lowenthal," Mallory had said excitedly, "as Moses studied my sketches, I pulled a piece of charcoal out of my pocket and sketched him.

"He said, 'Damn, that's good.' And he agreed to let me use his likeness for the mural."

From then on Mallory, captivated by his confidence as well as his prowess on the basketball court, had done sketch after sketch of him, until he became the central part of her mural.

And from the time Moses' image became a part of her montage, the wall remained graffiti free. As the work on the mural progressed, the number of sidewalk spectators grew. Several days later, she had been concentrating on her work when one of the younger children watching said excitedly, "It's the Judge." Conversation around her had stopped. She had looked up to see Moses standing and watching. The other kids stood in a half circle, a respectful distance from him.

She stopped working and cleaned her brushes. The spectators moved on, but Moses had remained. She'd pulled her lunch out of a small cooler and offered him half of her sandwich. They sat on the curb and ate. The next day, he'd appeared with two slices of pizza.

Mallory hadn't grown up in a ghetto, but she knew the amount of energy it took for a kid to survive in a place like this. She too had struggled to survive in one foster home after another. The anger and frustration these kids lived with was all they had. She understood that. Most of the kids didn't plan for their futures because they figured they didn't have any. But in Moses, Mallory saw a kid who had something that mattered. He had plans for his future.

They'd begun having lunch together, either sandwiches that Mallory prepared at home or pizza or hot dogs that Moses picked up. Most of the time they ate in silence, but little by little, as they began to trust each other, bits of their stories came out. And their friendship grew. He could be a painter, Mallory thought. She could see the promise in him each time she studied his basketball. He carried an assortment of felt tipped Sharpies in his pocket, and when he wasn't on a basketball court, or studying in the library, he was drawing on the ball. The markers wore off on the court, so he was constantly drawing new designs.

Monday, July 12
Chapter 9

On Monday, at exactly seven A.M., Willard Thompson arrived at the hospital in a suit and tie. Even a hospital orderly needed clearance which involved fingerprint checks. Having a record, Thompson would not have been accepted, so he had become a volunteer. Still, he was supposed to sign in.

"Looking good." The security guard said turning the time sheet book to him.

"Hot date tonight. Brought you some coffee, Chuck," Thompson said, handing the guard a cup. Then, juggling the bag with the remaining cup in one hand, and the satchel he carried daily in his other, he reached for the pen. His coffee spilled.

"Damn," Thompson said, making a big show of wiping his jacket. "It's going to stain unless I get it rinsed off quick."

"Go on. Don't worry about this," Chuck waved him through without the customary sign-in.

"Sure thing. Thanks." Thompson headed for the elevator, a smile plastered on his face. It had been easy to get chummy with the security guard—and get access to his master key. Chuck had a habit of leaving his keys on the table in the employees' lounge when he went to the john. Previously, Thompson had pulled a piece of wax he'd brought with him out of his pocket, and made a mold of the key.

Dividing his time among some of the Brooklyn hospitals—running errands, shuttling patients to various treatments, doing whatever paperwork was asked of him—he had made himself indispensable to the various departments, until no one questioned his presence.

Once in the elevator, Thompson pushed eight: Obstetrics. He pulled his beige volunteer's jacket from the satchel and, not wanting to call more attention to himself than necessary, slipped it on over his suit jacket. He hated that jacket, hated the whole volunteer business, but it had served him well, giving him access to whatever he needed. He checked his watch.

The night nurses, as usual, paid little attention to him, even though he had come in an hour and a half before the volunteers normally did. They had rounds to complete before their shifts ended and the morning shift came on. Thompson had counted on this. The desk nurse, deep in conversation with an aide, barely nodded as he walked by.

Using his copy of the master key now, he opened the door to Dr. Pusitari's office. A fast look at the doctor's meticulous date book confirmed what Thompson already knew: today he was giving a lecture on Fetal Toxic Syndrome. Eight A.M. at the Downstate Medical Center. He had three scheduled deliveries later in the day, and six scheduled appointments in between. McGill's had been one of those—it was still in the book, but he knew she wouldn't show.

When he had placed the call, last Friday, he'd stressed how tight Dr. Pusitari's day was going to be, and asked if she wouldn't mind coming in early on Monday. She'd assured him that she'd be in at seven-thirty.

Thompson had become proficient, his timing impeccable. He would do what he needed to do when the woman came in, and be gone before Dr. Pusitari returned to his office. Then he'd finish his job with her that night at his place.

While he waited for McGill, he went through his old satchel and pulled out the drugs he'd brought with him to induce her labor. He had only a bit left now from the stash he'd accumulated over the years, but it would see him through until he was out of this racket.

He removed his volunteer's jacket, and straightened his suit jacket and tie. Then he added a stethoscope for authenticity, and waited for his patient. Right on time, as he had requested, she arrived.

Later that night, as he'd expected, the call came in. The girl was ready to deliver.

Chapter 10

Frank Assanato had been thirty-one when he'd been convicted of manslaughter. The lawyer had appealed, and the charges were eventually overturned, but when he got out two years later, he looked close to sixty. And, in the twelve years since, he had never had a restful night's sleep.

Frank Assanato's sister called him every night at eleven. If the phone rang at any other time, he cringed. The nervous twitch began even before he heard the gravelly voice of the lawyer's associate. It traveled from the corner of his mouth to his eye. Beads of perspiration formed on his upper lip. And the excruciating pain returned.

He raised his hand to the right side of his head, where his ear had been, pressing hard to the prosthetic one, trying to ward off the migraine and the nausea that always followed these calls. But what could he do? He knew he would never have gotten out of prison alive without that lawyer's help. Child killers didn't survive long in the big house. He hadn't meant for it to happen. He'd loved that kid. Hell, he was Ralphie's godfather, for Christ's sake.

Every few months, the gravelly voice called just to remind him that he owed the lawyer big time. Then, about eight months ago, he called in his marker.

The call came in at midnight and the terror of jail came rushing back to Frank. He could hear the tormenting whispers, *"Kid killers die slowly."* He had been afraid to sleep, afraid to eat, afraid to go to the john. First they broke his leg. Then one day, they'd grabbed him in the shower and held him down. The guy they called the Cutter sliced off his ear. *"A piece at a time, and you'll never know when the next piece is coming off,"* he'd whispered as Frank lay in a pool of bloody water.

There was no doubt, Frank owed the lawyer. He was more than willing to do what was asked of him. He had been told that no one would get hurt. "It's for an insurance claim. I just want you to adjust the oven so's it's leaking some gas. No big deal," the voice on the phone assured him. "You'll find the key case on the ledge above the door on the side of the stoop. When you finish the job, put the key case in the envelope you'll find under the green trash can, and drop it in the mail."

Frank found the key case just where he had been told to look. He had gone into the kitchen. The heat was on. The windows were closed. He had hurried through his assignment and left, locking the door behind him and dropping the keys in the mail as instructed.

Then he read in the paper the very next day about a gas explosion, and that this guy was found dead in that same house. An accident, the paper said. Damn. He knew it was no accident, but who could he tell?

Although the lawyer's associate had already called in his marker, he continued to call and, each time his phone rang, Frank cringed anew.

"You're not finished yet. There is another job to do," the voice said.

"I won't have to hurt anyone, will I? Please, I can't do that. You said no one would get hurt before."

"Frankie, Frankie, did we ask you to hurt anyone? It was an accident, like the papers said. I'll call you when I need you."

And a few days later, the associate did.

Frank Assanato heard the jarring ring of his telephone and was immediately awake—and fearful again. He stared at the phone as it rang, and then rang again a second time, a third, and a fourth. He took a deep breath. The red numbers on his bedside clock read 11:50 P.M. It couldn't be his sister. He'd spoken to her at eleven.

He pulled himself up to a sitting position and stared at the phone. The nervous twitch began. His hand trembled. Although a cool breeze blew through the open window, his shirt—damp with perspiration—clung to him. His right hand went to the right side of his head. The excruciating pain, the terror in jail, everything came rushing back to him all over again.

A fifth ring, and then a sixth. He lifted the receiver, and slowly put it to his left ear.

"Hello, Frankie. How's our boy?" The same voice: gravelly, slow, precise. The lawyer's associate. Never the lawyer. Always his associate.

"No. I'm not doing anything else. You promised me no one would get hurt the last time."

"Frankie, Frankie, accidents happen. You of all people should know that."

"No. No more. You said *one* thing. All I had to do was *one* thing, and I did it. And I put the key case in the padded envelope and mailed it, like you said."

"Now Frankie." The voice became even more precise. "How is that sister of yours?"

"You leave Charlotte alone."

"If she has an accident…"

Frank held his breath. His heartbeat quickened. He knew there was more to come. "By the way," the voice resumed in the same slow, controlled way, "how is that dog of your sister's? Jack, I believe she calls him?"

"You go near my sister or her dog and I'll…"

"You'll what? You'll do nothing," The voice held steady. "I just happen to have the key case from your last uh, how shall we say it— adventure? You should be more careful where you leave your fingerprints. Do you think the authorities might like to see it…?"

Frank sighed, but said nothing. He slumped down in his bed and swallowed hard, knowing he'd been beaten. "I'm listening. I'm ready," he said. He picked up a piece of paper and jotted down the instructions, then the address, and then the name: Mallory McGill.

"Wait," he said. "Ocean View Avenue to East 17th and Avenue M in ten minutes? That's impossible."

"Be there." The line went dead.

Fear started his adrenaline flowing. He grabbed his car keys and slipped on his moccasins. Rather than wait for the elevator, he ran down four flights of stairs. Pain shot through his leg. It had never been set properly in prison. He limped swiftly through the double doors of the lobby and across the pitiful lawn in front of the building. Then he jumped over the low hedge to his car at the curb. He went through seven red lights, swerved twice to avoid pedestrians crossing the street, and barely missed three oncoming cars. Nine minutes later, Frank turned his old Ford onto East 17th Street.

The heavy foliage on the tree-lined street blocked the light of the lamp posts, and he cursed that he had to slow down to look for the address. He saw her standing near the curb or, more precisely, bent over and leaning against the hood of a parked car. "Ms. McGill?" Frank asked, but he was sure it was her. He'd been told to look for a pregnant broad, and she was real pregnant.

"Yes, that's me," Mallory gasped in the midst of a contraction.

"I'm here to pick you up." He looked around as he got out of the car to help her in. The street was empty except for an old guy sitting at a window. "Act nonchalant," he said to himself, and he waved at the man. But his wave was not returned.

He opened the rear passenger door, and his passenger climbed slowly into the back seat, her loud, controlled breathing, that of a woman in labor. Frank drove west on Avenue M, then turned South on Ocean Parkway.

"Turn here. Here's the hospital," the girl said, but he drove past Coney Island Hospital.

"Stop," she said. "Please."

He continued driving.

"You passed the hospital. Oh God…" Her pleas became screams, broken only by shrieks, as one contraction hit and then another. She tried to open the door as he slowed for a light, but the child proof safety lock prevented her from doing that. Only he could open it from the front. He felt sorry for the girl, but he had his orders. He continued driving. It would be up to the guy he was bringing her to to calm her. She reached for him from the back seat. He jammed on the break. He'd only meant to push her away, but he shoved her too hard. She hit her head against the window pane and got so quiet.

Afraid he'd killed her, Frank drove faster. He turned right, just off Surf Avenue, and found the house, the first one after the empty lot on the right side of the street. The street light flickered. The street was empty except for an old blue Chevy parked in front of the house.

Locking the girl in the car, he hurried down the alley and knocked on the side door as he'd been instructed. Three knocks. A space. Two more knocks.

Thompson opened the door. Carrying a lightweight tarp and a hypodermic needle, he followed Frank back to the car. He looked both ways and then, needle in position, signaled for Frank to open the rear door.

The unconscious girl lay slumped in the seat. Thompson looked at Frank questioningly.

"There was, umm, a little accident. She banged her head," he said.

The man pushed Frank aside and put his fingers on her neck. "Good," he said, finding her pulse. "No need for this." He capped the hypodermic and slipped it into his pocket. Then pulled a small flashlight from another pocket, lifted Mallory's eyelid, and shined the light back and forth in her eye.

"She's all right. Bring her in."

Frank reached behind the girl, and, clasping his arms around her body, pulled her from the car. Thompson quickly threw the tarp over her. Together, they half dragged, half carried her down the alley. The tarp slipped off.

"Hurry, cover her," Thompson ordered.

Frank lowered her to the ground, retrieved the tarp and covered her again. Then, together they dragged the girl up the three steps and into the house.

In the one dim light Frank could make out a kitchen sink, a counter, and a refrigerator. In the center he saw an examination table complete with stirrups, and beside that, some sort of monitor like he'd seen in his doctor's office. He tripped over one of those adjustable stands that doctors hang drip bottles from, and banged his head on a low hanging light above the table. "What is this place?"

"Help me lift her onto the table, and mind your own business."

"Look, mister, I'm just trying to make conversation. I don't give a shit what you do in here. If I didn't have a fucking debt to pay off, I wouldn't be playing delivery man."

"Yeah… well, buddy, wait in your car. I'll call you when I'm finished," Thompson said with a false bravado.

"It's Frank to you."

Thompson slammed the door behind Frank and locked it. Only then did he switch on the bright light that hung over the table.

Quickly, he positioned the woman's feet in the stirrups, spreading them wide apart and strapping them in place to allow him an unobstructed view and easy access for the delivery. After pulling up her dress, and cutting off her underpants, he placed a stretchable band around her belly and tucked a fetal monitor underneath it.

Satisfied that the fetal heartbeat and uterine contractions were good, he found a vein on her arm, and taped the intravenous needle in place. He added a mixture of morphine-scopolamine to the glucose solution. Twilight sleep would keep her manageable and fog her memory if she came back to consciousness while he was working on her.

The contractions were coming fast now. Three minutes apart, then two. Thompson lathered up his hands and arms and scrubbed them again. He had a pile of clean towels and sheets standing nearby—compliments of Coney Island Hospital. He checked the woman's cervix. She had dilated to 10 centimeters. The baby's head was in position, and her birth canal was widening. Her pelvis was a good size The head crowned. Then was out. As he supported it, there was a gush of reddish liquid, and the rest of the baby's body slid out. Thompson clamped off and cut the cord.

Holding the infant with its head angled down, he inserted the tip of a compressed bulbous tube, and suctioned mucus from its throat. Quickly, he cleared the tube, and repeated the procedure two more times. The baby gave a weak, squeaky cry. The woman whimpered and raised her head. He put the baby down beside her, and injected Valium into the tube that dripped a clear liquid into her arm. Her head fell back to the table, and she was silent again. Efficiently, he dropped antiseptic solution into the baby's eyes, then bathed her with warm mineral oil. He diapered her, wrapped her securely in a receiving blanket, and put a little cap on her head to keep the warmth in her body.

The one part of the hospital routine he no longer followed was the foot-printing and labeling of the baby. Before turning his attention back to the mother, he carried the baby to a small room and placed it in an incubator.

Then he returned to the woman. Usually minutes after giving birth, the uterus begins to contract again. Those first few contractions separate the placenta from the uterine wall. That wasn't happening. He applied gentle pressure over her pelvic bone, but that did nothing to start it.

Frank had been sitting in the car. More than an hour passed, and then another, while he waited. His leg cramped, and he stepped out to ease the cramp. Up the deserted block he walked, past a ramshackle row of houses and trash-strewn lots, and back again. Crumbled buildings and more vacant lots lined the other side of the street. The bright moonlight did little to dispel the gloom.

He leaned against his car and studied the windows of the doctor's house. Those on the ground floor were boarded up. The windows on the second and third floors were dark. He walked noiselessly down the alley. At the side door where he'd brought the pregnant woman, he listened, but heard nothing. He went round to the rear, and as he backed away to better see the house, he tripped over an empty bucket half buried in the tall weeds. With a thud, he fell to the ground.

Thompson heard the noise and looked up. A cat growled, and another screeched back. He went back to applying gentle pressure over the girl's pelvic bone. Nothing was happening. He couldn't wait. Although it meant an increased risk of bleeding, he had to get her out of his place. He removed the fetal monitor, unstrapped her legs, and pulled off the tape that held the needle. The woman moved, and the needle gashed her arm.

After making a mad dash back to the car, Frank was feigning sleep when, moments later, Thompson knocked on the window, motioning him back to the door at the side of the house. The woman, still out of it, was lying on the table. Frank looked from her to the bundle of bloody sheets on the floor. He heard a baby cry. "What the…"

Thompson gave him a piercing look.

"I ain't seen nothing. I ain't heard nothing," Frank said.

Between them, the two men carried Mallory McGill back to the car.

"You know what you've been instructed to do with her. Now get out of here."

Frank drove west on Neptune Avenue, then turned right on Bayview until he was almost at the end. He backed onto the service road, stopping where the road came closest to the creek, and dragged the woman from the car. The back seat was covered with blood. He wiped the seat with the woman's sweater, which had fallen to the floor. Then he balled it up and tossed it toward the creek.

Although the night had cooled, and it had begun to rain, by the time he found a parking space near his place, sweat ran profusely down his forehead. He raised his arm and wiped his face on his shirt sleeve. His hand moved to the right side of his head. Damn. His ear prosthesis was missing.

He searched the car; feeling between the seats, under them, pulling up the mats. Nothing. He couldn't chance going back to the creek to look for it. Someone might have found the girl by now. The place could be swarming with cops. He drove back to the house off Surf Avenue, and retraced his steps into the alley they'd dragged the woman through. No sign of the ear.

Shit. It had cost him a fortune. Maybe he'd lost it in the back yard. He tiptoed into the yard and, on his hands and knees, felt around through the weeds where he had fallen—no luck. He'd have to eat the loss.

As he got up from the ground to leave, he noticed a sliver of light coming through a crack high in the board covering the window. He climbed onto the bucket and peered in.

An infant, not much larger than a football, lay quietly in the doctor's arm as he talked on his phone. Frank put his good ear to the crack to listen.

"Dantano, the shipment's in. It's pink and in excellent condition, You'll have it tomorrow afternoon. The price we agreed on." Frank turned to look into the crack in the board. The doctor hung up the phone. "No more pay-backs after you," he said to the infant. "That lawyer will never find me. Dantano will never find me. I won't have to do anyone's dirty work ever again. In forty-eight hours, I'll be on a flight to Alaska."

Frank had just fallen into another restless sleep when the phone rang.

"You did good, Frankie. Reeeaaallll good," the gravelly voice, slow and precise, said. Then the phone clicked off before Frank had a chance to say anything.

Seconds later, it rang again. "What the fuck do you want now!" he screamed into the receiver.

"Frank, it's me, Charlotte," came the frightened voice of his sister.

"I'm sorry. I thought you were some asshole who's been bothering me." Then, realizing that it was 5 A.M., he sat up. "What's wrong? Why are you calling so early?"

Charlotte was crying.

"What is it? Did something happen to Murray, or Jack?"

"No. They're fine. I wasn't going to tell you but I've been up all night. Oh Frank, our application came back from the adoption agency. Denied. We're too old."

"Oh no. Maybe another agency?"

"We've tried them all. It's no use."

Frank closed his eyes, but nothing could erase the image of his sister sitting all alone in the courtroom. She hadn't been able to look at him during his trial, but when the judge announced the verdict of manslaughter, it was she who had come to his defense. "Please, your honor, I'm sure he didn't mean to, didn't mean to… kill my baby." Charlotte said, her last words barely audible.

Her child, his nephew and godson, had died because of him. He'd unlocked the window. And yet his sister had defended him. And when he was sent to Sing Sing Correctional Facility, a maximum security prison, she drove up to Ossining, New York, more than fifty miles each way, every week, to visit him.

Frank hadn't touched a bottle since that night. He'd applied to school, and two years later had become an EMT. The job of an Emergency Medical Technician was stressful, and that was exactly what he needed. No time to remember the past.

He bought Charlotte a little house in Jackson Heights. And got her a golden retriever. Jack, she called it, after a favorite teacher of hers. She loved the dog. He was like her shadow. But Jack didn't take the place of Ralphie, her dead child. Nothing could. There was no way he could make up to his sister for the terrible loss he had caused her. Then, a couple of years ago, she met this guy Murray and married him. They'd moved to Niagara Falls, and had been trying to adopt a baby ever since.

"Listen, I've got vacation time coming. I'll drive up on Saturday, and we'll spend a few days together. We'll figure something out. Anyway, it's about time you and Murray showed me around that town of yours."

He lay in bed after the phone call, remembering that day he'd messed up his sister's life—the day little Ralphie had died.

The conversation he'd had with his sister was still clear in his head.

It was he who had urged her to start going out after her husband died. "You did all you could for Pete with his long illness. Now he's gone," he'd told Charlotte. "You can't let little Ralphie become your whole life. You have to get out. Meet people."

She had been hesitant. The only one who ever watched her son was her neighbor, but the woman had moved to Florida.

"I'll babysit," he had said.

Charlotte finally consented. She left Frank with a list: what to give his godson for snacks, his favorite stories, his bedtime. She also left a list of emergency telephone numbers before she'd gone to meet her friends for the evening.

Frank played cars with little Ralphie, read him a story, and then put him to bed. How was he to know a two-year-old kid could climb out of a crib?

The idea came to him suddenly after three hours of tossing and turning in bed. He could fix things. Make her happy again.

He pulled on his sweats and Nikes. Rummaging through his drawer, he found his long-haired wig, the one he wore before he'd raised the dough to have the prosthesis made. It went over his ears, or where his ear would have been, and banded at the nape of his neck. He pulled apart his closet until he found his old duffel bag: about 20 inches long, and with a zipper the length of the top. It would do just fine.

"Hope it's still there, hope it's still there," he repeated over and over, as he drove back to Coney Island. It was early morning, and the air was still. Traffic was light. The game booths on Surf Avenue were gated, and the small food concessions closed. The Wonder Wheel stood immobile, majestic above the other rides. Nathan's was just opening. The stadium parking lot was empty. He turned off Surf and slowly cruised past the house he had been to only hours before. The same blue car was parked in front of the house.

Frank parked around the corner and took the bag from the trunk. He stopped at a grocery store and bought a newspaper. Across the street from the house, someone had ripped the bottom out of a plastic crate and nailed it high up on a light post. A couple of teens were tossing a ball through the improvised basketball hoop to the noise of a loud boom box.

At a nearby wall, Frank put the bag down and raised the paper in front of him—just like he'd seen detectives do in hundreds of TV shows.

Pretending to read, he anxiously watched the house through a small hole he'd torn in the front page. All he could do was hope that the man would leave.

Ever since those years on skid row, when he'd let them go, Thompson had trouble with his teeth; infections, abscesses. The day before, he'd woken with a horrible toothache. Usually Vicodin helped, but not this time. Now his cheek and neck were swollen, and he was suffering an excruciating migraine. This abscess was bad. He could tell the signs. He had to have the pus drained immediately. Past patients of his had had their hearts affected by infections milder than this.

He hated leaving the baby unattended. The windows were boarded up, but how soundproof were they, especially at the front of the house? What if someone heard her crying? He moved the incubator out of the bedroom, through the kitchen, and into a tiny closet. It was plugged in and working fine. Still, for good measure, he hooked up the emergency generator, and left the door to the closet slightly ajar.

All of the baby's vital signs were good. He gave her a bottle and changed her diaper. Then, he picked her up and held her close to him. "I'll be back soon," he said. "The dentist will be in at ten. And tomorrow you'll have a brand new home."

Tuesday, July 13
Chapter 11

The kids continued shooting baskets and Frank continued watching and waiting, his nerves wearing thin. Then the door in the alley opened. The guy he'd delivered the girl to came out carrying a black plastic trash bag in the crook of his arm. The bag was about the size of a new born baby. "Oh shit. No. He couldn't have…" Frank punched the wall.

An instant later, a large white recycling truck came to a halt, blocking Frank's view. He paced from the wall to the curb and then back again. "Hurry it up, fucker," he muttered under his breath. The truck moved on. The blue car was gone, and so was the guy. A blue recycling can lay on its side, empty, but a regular trash can remained standing, its lid undisturbed. Frank balled up the newspaper, grabbed his bag, and hurried across the street. He hesitated for a moment before opening the trash can. The stench was horrific, the plastic bag tucked in with the garbage. He held his breath as he gingerly moved the garbage. Then he untwisted the tie and peered inside the bag. An audible sigh escaped his lips.

The bag held an empty quart-sized paint can, torn, paint-splattered paper, and sheets. He could make out the words Coney Island Hospital on the edge of the cloth. "So he hid the blood under red paint. Smart guy," Frank said to himself.

He looked across the street. The kids with the boom box were engrossed in their game. He hurried into the alley, then looked back again. The side door could too easily be seen. So, ignoring the pain that shot through his leg, he ran past it and to the rear of the house.

He pulled out the crowbar he'd brought in his duffel bag. The nail screeched as he pried it loose from the largest board covering one of the windows. He stopped to listen for the boys. Had they heard? No. Their music blaring from across the street drowned out everything. He removed more nails, until the board swung to the side on the one remaining nail. Quickly he raised the window, reached inside, and put his bag on the sink below it. Then he hoisted himself over the sill and onto the kitchen sink. The board slid back into place, enveloping him in darkness.

At first he heard only a quiet hum. The refrigerator. Frank took his flashlight from his bag and switched it on. The room was empty. No baby. He shined the light rapidly along the walls. To his left was the side door bolted from the outside. Across the room, opposite the window, were two doors. He opened the first. A mattress leaned against a wall in the otherwise empty room. He opened the second door to a room that looked like a store room. Nothing but old furniture. "Fuck," he said, kicking the door.

He returned to the kitchen, shining his light frantically about. A couple of lines led from an outlet to a smaller door across from the side door. He yanked open the door. Shelves with some food goods showed it to be a pantry, but squeezed in the center sat an incubator. And a newborn baby lay sleeping in it. He let out the breath he didn't realize he'd been holding in.

Moving fast, Frank grabbed some diapers and receiving blankets, and stuffed them into the bottom of the duffle bag. The baby began to cry as he picked her up. "Oh hell, what do I do now? I can't have you crying in a bag." He opened the refrigerator and pulled out a bottle of formula. Three sips and the baby fell asleep, the nipple still in her mouth. Frank wrapped her in a towel he'd brought with him and tucked her gently into the bag on top of the things he'd packed earlier. He grabbed the rest of the bottles of formula and stuffed them into his large sweatshirt pockets.

He slid the board away, and climbed onto the sink and then out the window, before reaching in and lifting out the bag he'd left on the counter. Quickly, he closed the window and replaced the board. Avoiding the alley, where he might be noticed, he cut through the broken fence to the next yard and, sweat pouring from his face, he limped back to his car around the corner.

Just as he put his duffle bag into the front seat, the Chevy—the one he'd seen parked in front of Thompson's place earlier—rounded the corner. Frank lowered his head, pretending to tie his shoelace, until it passed. He jumped into the driver's seat and drove home slowly, staying under the speed limit, one hand on the wheel and one on the bag beside him. The little thing woke and wiggled in the duffel bag.

Prison had done a number on Frank. He'd become fearful, apprehensive, and extremely cautious. He changed apartments more often than some people cleaned theirs. But it wasn't difficult to move. After prison life, his needs were minimal; a mattress, a television, a chair, and a snack table, and these he moved himself. His newest landlord had given him permission to look through the basement for any additional furniture previous tenants might have left. He'd found a dresser, a bed frame, and a night stand.

It was cold in the apartment when Frank returned with the baby. The landlord hadn't turned the heat on yet. So Frank turned on his oven to warm the room. He emptied a drawer from the dresser and padded it with a folded towel. Then he lined it with a blanket and put the make-shift crib on his chair near the open oven door.

As he lifted her out of his satchel, the baby began to cry. Holding her awkwardly, Frank gave her one of the bottles of formula he'd put in his pocket. She latched onto the nipple and sucked.

"Oh baby. I never did anything like this before," Frank said. His foot jerked rapidly up and down. He pressed his hand to his knee, but couldn't control the nervous twitch. "I sure could use a drink. No. I won't. I haven't touched the stuff since the night little Ralphie died."

The baby looked up at him with curious eyes.

"I didn't mean to hurt him. Honest. I loved that kid. He was sleeping when I opened the window. Charlotte had some sort of kid proof lock on it, but I forced it open. I had to. My sister disapproved of alcohol in her place, and she'd have smelled it when she got home.

"It was going to be a quiet evening. Just me and Johnny Walker. I figured, what the heck, I was spending the night on the couch anyway. It wasn't like I was going to be out on the roads driving."

Frank placed the baby in the make-shift crib. She continued to stare at him with wizened eyes.

"Stop looking at me like that. It wasn't my fault. The kid must have gotten up, climbed onto the sill. Next thing I knew, there was a pounding on the door. I heard people screaming. Honest to God, I didn't know what happened until the neighbors told me that Ralphie was lying dead on the sidewalk four floors down."

Chapter 12

The dentist's novocaine had done wonders. Thompson was feeling no pain as he unlocked the door to the quiet hum of the refrigerator. He turned on the light and walked into the pantry-turned-nursery. The incubator was empty. Unable to believe his own eyes, he ran his hand over the small mattress. He'd been gone less than two hours.

He ran out of the side door, to the front of the house. He looked down the street to one corner, and then to the other, but saw no one. He walked back to his house fuming. "Fuck. Fuck. Fuck. All of my plans," his fist slammed into the hood of his car. "Who the hell could have done this?"

There was a triple dead bolt on the door, and he had the only keys. He walked around the house checking his boarded up windows. They were still covered. In the yard, he ran his fingers over the edge of a board. A fresh splinter pierced his thumb. The board had been pried open.

Not a soul was out except those damn kids and their boom box across the street. "Hey you guys," he called, but they ignored him until he stomped across the street and grabbed their ball.

"What the fuck you think you're doing, man?"

He grabbed the arm of the bigger kid and twisted it. "When I talk to you punks, you answer. You got that?"

"Yeah mister. I got it."

"You see anyone around here earlier?"

"Not me."

"Me either."

Thompson pulled a twenty-dollar bill out of his pocket. "Maybe this will refresh your memories."

"There was a guy with a newspaper." The kid stopped rubbing his arm and went for the bill. Thompson pulled it back.

"A funny looking dude—long hair. Looked like a wig."

"Give me more," Thompson said, waving the bill in front of them.

"He had a some sort of a bag, and he was reading a paper."

"For a long time," the smaller kid added.

"Then what'd he do?"

"He crossed the street. I think he threw his paper in your garbage can. Oh yeah. He was limping. That's all we saw. Honest."

"Limping? That motherfucker." Thompson handed the shorter kid the twenty.

"So blackmail's your game," he said to himself as he stomped back across the street. "We'll just see if it pays."

Grabbing his tool box, he pounded one nail after another into the board that had been forced open. "Two can play your game." He pounded the nails harder and harder. "I got your license plate."

Just as he came back into his place, the phone rang. He knew it would be Dantano. "I've had a little problem. The package, um, got misplaced."

"I don't want any crap from you. I want that package or a replacement within two days. This one's earmarked for a good cash customer. If you're trying to hit me up for more dough, your life won't be worth shit. I'll take you apart a piece at a time."

Thompson broke into a sweat. No one tangled with Dantano. He knew that. When they'd first started doing business together, Dantano had left him a gift of a severed hand. With it was a note that said, "This poor bastard thought he could put something over on me. Don't you try."

"You aren't trying to fuck with me, are you?"

"No. No. You'll get your… package."

"I'll be watching you until I do."

Thompson knew Dantano meant what he said. He couldn't leave until he turned over a baby.

Just then he heard Dora, his feeble-minded neighbor, talking to herself as she ambled through his yard. "Let me get back to you. I need to check something."

Dora was pregnant. He knew it.

Thompson had judged the girl to be about eighteen or nineteen, but it was difficult for him to be certain, because of her immense size. She spent her days eating sweets on the front steps. He'd heard the neighborhood boys rapping, "Dora, Dora, you're one fine bitch. Take this candy and show us your tits." And he'd seen Dora open her shirt and eagerly take the candy. On several occasions, he'd watched from behind the broken fence as the neighborhood boys fingered her nipples, then more aggressively groped at her breasts, while the childlike woman delighted in the bits of chocolate. And he'd seen older boys, using candy as a lure, lead her to the back of the house and do more than just touch her.

The dark color of the areolas around her nipples, and the fullness of her white breasts had made him almost certain that she was pregnant. Still, because of her girth, he hadn't been completely sure. If she was expecting, he might have another baby to sell and extra, easy cash. So he had examined her just last week.

It had been easy. He'd purchased a bag of candies and, holding it out to her, had said, "Come on, Dora, and I'll give you candy."

"Dora like candy," she said, and followed him docilely into his kitchen.

He bolted the door. "Now take off your underpants so we can play a nice game."

With the offer of a few M&Ms, she obediently did as she was told. Another few M&Ms, and she climbed onto the examination table, lied down, and allowed him to put her feet into the stirrups. "You're such a good girl." he said, handing her a peppermint stick. She sucked happily on the candy as he spread her ample thighs, inserted the fingers of one hand into her vagina, and palpitated her stomach with his other hand.

The internal had confirmed Thompson's suspicions. Dora was pregnant. Almost eight months. "In another month, I'll bring you back here. You'll give me something I want, and I'll give you more candy. Won't that be nice?"

Now, however, with Dantano on his tail, he had no choice. The fetus had seemed to be only about four or five pounds, but he couldn't wait. It would have to be enough. He looked at his watch. Noon. He wouldn't have enough time to induce her now, but tomorrow, Wednesday, was a good day. The girl's father worked six days a week. On Wednesdays he left his house at eight A.M. and returned twelve-hours later. Thompson would have to do it then. Thursday was the father's day off. He spent that either in the house or on his porch with a couple of six packs.

As soon as her father left for work the following morning, Thompson enticed Dora over to his house with a bag of sweets, as he had the previous week. Before he'd had time to lock the door, she had taken off her underpants and held out her plump hand. "Candy now."

Acting quickly, he got her into position on the table, pulled up her dress, and prepared a line. He gave her a tiny piece of chocolate. "If you're a good girl you can have another soon," he said, taping her arm to her side to keep it still.

She lay on the table docilely, chewing on the morsel as he efficiently found her vein, swabbed the spot, and stuck her with a needle. Before she could cry out, he stuffed another bit of chocolate into her mouth. He taped the intravenous needle in place and began the drip. Along with the mixture of morphine-scopolamine which would induce twilight sleep, he'd added Pitocin to start her uterine contractions.

Thompson observed her closely with a fetal monitor, gradually increasing the dose while keeping her under. Six hours later, her cervix was fully dilated. He slipped on a pair of surgical gloves.

As the baby's head came into view, he could see Dora's vagina beginning to tear. He contemplated doing an episiotomy to enlarge the opening and speed the delivery, but then he'd have to stitch the incision. No. He wanted no signs that a doctor had anything to do with this birth.

The small baby emerged silent. A boy.

Swiftly, he cleared the baby's lungs, and was thanked with a squeaky cry. Placing him in the incubator, he hurried back to finish with Dora. Minutes after giving birth, her uterus began to contract, and with a little pressure, her placenta separated from her uterine wall. He ran oxytocin, ten units into a liter of IV fluids, to encourage her uterus to contract more. He checked the clock, knowing he had to get her back home before her father had a clue as to what had happened.

An hour later, using a great deal of strength, he tugged her up to a sitting position and pulled her off the table. The promise of a bag of M&Ms started her moving and, supporting her girth, he led her through the broken fence that had once separated the houses and to the back door of her house, which he'd noted previously, was always unlocked. He got her to the couch and tightly wrapped her legs in a blanket, counting on her more than adequate thighs to curtail any post-delivery bleeding.

After a large scotch, he made his phone call to Dantano. "Your replacement package is ready. Only it came in blue, small but functional."

"I like blue. The line?"

Thompson didn't have a clue as to whether this baby might be feeble minded like its mother, but by the time anyone who got the kid could have it tested—three months was when they did that sort of stuff—he'd be long gone. "Well bred; university students, Phi Beta Kappas. It was a last-minute decision," he said. Figuring in a few more days the baby would be more stable, he said, "I'll get the package to you on Saturday."

"You don't tell me nothing. I tell you. Understand? I want it tomorrow. Thursday."

"That's too soon. He was just born," Thompson protested.

"Tomorrow," Dantano said, and hung up the phone.

Wednesday, July 14
Chapter 13

At the precinct, Detective Sam Rothman licked his fingers, savoring the last bit of Rachel's blueberry muffin. Leaning back in his seat, he clasped his hands behind his head and lifted his feet to rest them on the desk, tilting his chair until it balanced precariously on the two rear legs. "Nice and quiet today. No phones ringing. Just the way I like it."

"What about the girl with the missing baby, and the body found in an alley in Coney Island," Cardello reminded him.

He picked up a wadded piece of paper from the pile beside his chair, took aim, and tossed it into the circular file across the room. "A piece of cake."

Desk Sergeant Lazaro kicked open the detectives' door. Rothman's chair slipped out from under him and he landed on the floor. "God damn it. Every nut case in the city is calling. What is it, a full moon or something?"

Unfazed by Lazaro's rantings, or Rothman's spill—and the obscenities that spilled from his mouth when he landed on the floor—Cardello continued sifting through her casework. "What's the latest, Sergeant," she asked without looking up from her papers.

"It's that Kesselman dame again. If she calls me one more time about those fuckin' cats of hers…" Lazaro's voice went up two octaves in an imitation of Mrs. Kesselman: "The upstairs neighbors don't have carpeting. Their footsteps are disturbing poor Snow Ball's nap. It's sooo distressing."

"She simply has to have her rest, you know." Cardello finished his sentence laughing. "It's your turn, Sam. I got the last wacko."

Rothman stood up and righted his chair. "OK. Next time she calls, I'll talk to her. "

"Good. This looney's yours." Satisfied, Lazaro headed for the door. "Oh," he turned back, "any word from the divers yet? The press got wind of the McGill case, and they're on my tail."

"None. They're still searching," Cardello said. "We're waiting to hear before we speak to the girl again."

"Come on, Sam. Get your ass in gear," Cardello said. "The Coney Island corpse isn't getting any warmer."

Rothman picked up a second missile and took aim. "The kid's dead. What's another few minutes?"

Although school was out for the summer, there was a break in the chain link fence, and a basketball game was in progress on the court.

Suddenly, as if on cue, the crowd began to thin out. Street kids could sense cops, even in plain clothes and, as Cardello and Rothman approached, they disbanded, one at a time, until only Moses remained in the school yard. Ignoring the approaching detectives, he continued to shoot the ball, making basket after basket, without a miss.

"Hey, you. Get over here," Cardello called.

Moses made another basket. "You wanna talk to me?"

"We do if you're the kid they call the Judge."

"I *am* the Judge."

Moses continued shooting until Cardello grabbed the ball, and made a basket. Moses, caught off guard by this woman, paused for an instant. Then he reached back and retrieved the ball. They played some one on one, until, winded, Cardello stopped to catch her breath. She turned the ball in her hand to study the unusual graffiti-like art that covered it.

"Most athletes initial their balls, or tag them, but this ball is a work of art. Actually nice. Real nice. You do this?"

"Yeah." Moses reclaimed his ball. "You're pretty good, mama."

"You're not so bad yourself. Why do they call you the Judge?"

"Cause I make the decisions. I keep the peace." He twirled the basketball on his index finger. "I'm the man here. You need supplies, I'm your supplier. You need a job done, I'm your arranger. You need answers, I'm your information man."

"Then answer me this, information man," Rothman, who had come closer to the two, pulled out a photo of the kid they'd found dead in Coney Island. "Do you know this guy?"

"Why you asking?"

"He was wearing a Lincoln High School senior ring." Rothman grabbed Moses' hand. "Just like yours. A schoolmate?"

Moses pulled his hand free and took the photo. He glanced at it for a second. "Yeah, I knew him. Name's Eduardo. Eduardo Gonzalez."

"Knew him," Cardello asked.

"Knew him. He dropped out of school a month or so ago."

"Where's he live?"

"How the hell should I know? Haven't seen him since. But shit, man," Moses said studying the photo more closely, "he looks dead."

"Very observant. This was taken at the morgue."

"How'd he get it?"

"Get what?"

Emphasizing each word, Moses said, "How. The. Fuck. Did. He. Die?"

"How do most junkies die? Shooting up. Bad stuff."

Holding Eduardo's photo in one hand, Moses dribbled his ball out of Cardello's reach.

Rothman grabbed the photo from Moses's hand. "Come on, Teri. We're not going to get anything else out of this kid."

"Come around any time. I'll spot ya' five," Moses called after Cardello, as the detectives headed off the court.

He dribbled for a few more minutes, keeping his eyes on the retreating detectives.

No sooner were they in their car when the other players emerged, as if out of nowhere. "Come on, Moses, pick your team," one of them urged.

"Nah. I got stuff I gotta do."

Moses had been to Eduardo's only once since he'd gotten his own place, but his memory was good, and he'd gotten the lay of the land on his first visit. His motto was, "You never know." It would be only a day or two, tops, before the cops got the address. He might just be able to salvage some stuff before they got there. So, after midnight, Moses made his way through the yards of the decaying houses, and jumped the fence into the yard of Eduardo's place. Actually, he could have just slipped through the decayed fence, but he believed in keeping in practice.

The few street lights that worked didn't much cut the dark of the yards, but the moonlight in the clear sky helped him to spot the fire escape ladder hanging off the ground. He jumped high enough to catch hold of the lowest rung—first try. Chinning, he raised himself until he could swing his legs up, and then climbed to the second floor landing. Staying close to the wall, he made his way up the steps to the third floor. With his trusty little knife, he pried the window open. In a flash, he was in the apartment. The moonlight filtered through the tattered shade, but he turned on his small penlight to get a better look. A mouse scurried away.

Just as he remembered, a soiled mattress sat in the middle of the floor, and discarded take-out containers and stale food littered the space around it. Only now, the pile of rubbish had grown. The stench of rotting food and unwashed bed linen caused him to scrunch up his nose.

"Damn, Eduardo, your place still looks like a shit hole. And it smells like one, too," Moses said to his dead friend. He wiped his hands on his jeans, and then pulled on the rubber gloves he carried with him.

Carefully, he shook out a filthy, smelly sheet, then picked up and shook a grease-stained pillow. Feathers floated out from the torn ticking. Next he went through the dirty clothes that littered the floor. He searched through the pockets of Eduardo's shirts and baggy jeans. Piece by piece, he examined each article for anything that might be of value. Anyone else might have missed the wad of tens in the lining of the hoodie, or the weed wrapped in foil in the toe of the grungiest sock, but Moses was thorough, and he was rewarded for his thoroughness.

In a half-full coffee can, he found Eduardo's St. Christopher's medal, the one he'd won in his church class when they were little kids. "Well hello, Mr. Saint Christopher. How'd you like to bring me a few bucks?" he said, buffing the medal against his black T-shirt. Then he looked at it again. "Oh, what the hell, your mama. Jesus man. Your poor mama. I'll get this to her." He pocketed the piece, and exited the way he had come, through the window.

He'd just jumped from the ladder to the ground when he heard the door in the alley unlatch. Sidling up to the corner of the house, he watched as a man placed a black plastic bag on the step and then locked his door. The man looked both ways before heading out of the alley with the bag.

"Curiouser and curiouser." Quietly, Moses quoted his favorite line from *Alice in Wonderland* as he followed the man. "Where would this dude be going at this hour of the night?" Three blocks later, the man stopped at a dumpster, reached in, and buried his little bundle right in the middle of the trash. Moses watched from behind a parked car. "What was wrong with your own trash can? What are you trying to hide?" Moses waited until the man headed back toward his place, then he hurried to the dumpster to check the contents of the mysterious package.

Thursday, July 15
Chapter 14

Mrs. Rollins placed a tray on the bedside table. "Wake up, Ms. McGill. It's time for breakfast."

Mallory pulled the covers over her head. "Please God, let the past two days have been a horrible nightmare." She reached down and tentatively touched her stomach. She felt the emptiness. The nightmare was real. She closed her eyes.

"Eat, child. Eat. You need your strength."

Mallory turned over and raised her head from the pillow. A glass of orange juice, buttered toast, and eggs—sunny side up—sat on the night table, illuminated in the dim lamplight.

Mrs. Rollins pulled open the drapes. Bright sunlight flooded the room. "I'll be back later."

Mallory pulled herself up and tried to force down a sip of juice and a bit of toast. The toast stuck in her throat. She laid down again and pulled the covers up.

From far away, a doorbell sounded.

Mrs. Rollins escorted the detectives into the parlor. "I've prepared a delicious plate of brownies for you. Help yourselves."

"That wasn't necessary."

"Please. I insist. I'll be right back with a nice pot of tea. Miss McGill will be down shortly."

"Sweet old woman," Rothman said.

"Mr. B," she knocked on Brad's office door, "the detectives you told me about are here." Then she headed to the kitchen.

True to her word, the housekeeper was back in a short time with the tea she had promised them, and a pot of coffee besides. "Mr. B only drinks coffee," she said by way of explanation.

Detective Cardello sat on the edge of the brocaded Chippendale sofa in the elegant room, a delicate dish of brownies perched on her knee. Rothman, in his rumpled beige suit, stood near the decorative fireplace.

He spread his hand over the brownies, holding them on the dish as he turned it over.

"Rosenthal china," Cardello said, saving him the trouble of reading the bottom of the dish.

Rothman put the dish of brownies on the ornately designed marble mantel, and ran his fingers along the cut facets of the large glass lion that stood proudly on it. He was about to pick it up when Brad walked into the room. "Swarovski, captured in twenty-four crystal pieces. Sits on a granite base," he said. "Very heavy."

"Real nice, Mr. Dawson," Rothman said, dropping his hands to his sides before reclaiming his dish of brownies from the mantel. "Law work must pay well."

"I'll get Ms. McGill," Brad said ignoring the detective's comment.

The knock on her door startled Mallory. "Yes," she said, briefly unsure of where she was, until see saw the uneaten breakfast Mrs. Rollins had brought earlier.

"It's Brad. The detectives are downstairs. They'd like to talk to you."

She'd fallen asleep in her clothes when Brad had brought her back from her apartment the night before. Now, without pausing to wash or brush her teeth, she slipped into her sneakers and hurried after him, her open laces flapping down the stairs. Once in the hallway, she pushed Brad aside and ran into the living room. "You found my baby. I knew you would. Where is she?"

Detective Rothman gestured toward the winged arm chair. "Have a seat, Ms. McGill."

Mallory stopped short. She lowered herself to the edge of the seat. Her hands fisted in her lap. She took a deep breath, "You're not going to tell me something bad, are you?"

"Ms. McGill, we haven't found your baby yet. We need to ask you some more questions."

"Questions?" Mallory jumped out of the chair. "Why aren't you out looking for her? Someone took her. Someone has my baby."

Brad stood behind her. He touched her shoulder reassuringly. "Please, Mallory, sit down. You need to answer the detectives' questions."

Mallory sat down again, still on the edge of the chair.

"What did you do on Monday, Ms. McGill," Cardello asked.

Mallory turned at the sound of her voice. She hadn't noticed the detective sitting on the sofa when she'd entered the room.

"I saw the doctor."

"Was that for a regular appointment?"

"Yes. It was supposed to be in the afternoon, but the service called and said the doctor would see me earlier."

"And then what did you do?"

"I had arranged to see a prospective client right after. In Mill Basin."

"What were you wearing?"

"A loose sun dress I'd made—not much else fit me."

"So being pregnant was, umm," Detective Cardello paused, searching for the right word, "…inconvenient, shall we say?"

"No!" Mallory shot back. "I love handwork. It was artsy: turquoise, chartreuse, burgundy. And people are more impressed with an artist who looks the part. I had appliqued it, and done fancy embroidery on the pockets."

Mallory patted her side, where a pocket might have been. She sighed. "Keith had given me a small gold medallion with an artist's palette etched on it. For luck, he told me. I always had it with me, in my pocket."

"All right. Now, when you left the doctor's office, you went to Mill Basin, and…" Cardello was noting everything on a small pad, "and who did you see there?"

"No. I felt funny after my examination. The doctor had given me some kind of a drip—for nutrition, he said. And the internal he gave me made me very uncomfortable, so I canceled my appointment and went home instead. I rested for most of the day."

"And in the evening? What did you do then?"

"I felt better then. I spent the early part of the evening painting, working on a commissioned portrait."

"Until what time was that?"

"I can't say exactly…" anger rose in Mallory. "What does all of this have to do with finding my baby?"

"Mallory, please. Just answer the questions," Brad said gently.

"I'd been working for some time. I'd just opened a tube of cobalt blue to add to my pallet when that first contraction jolted me. It was so strong that I clenched my fists. The color gushed out of the tube and onto the floor." Mallory looked at her hands, still tinged with blue. She held the palms up for the detectives to see. "But it was too soon. I wasn't due for another two weeks. I called Brad." She turned toward Dawson. "You sent a driver to get me."

"Mallory, think clearly. I play racquetball on Monday nights. You know that. And you know that if I had been home, I'd have come myself. I wouldn't have sent someone else."

"Yes. No. Wait." Confused, Mallory raised her hands to her temple. "Mrs. Rollins—I spoke to Mrs. Rollins. She said you weren't home. *She* sent a car. I remember now. It was Mrs. Rollins. She said she'd have your driver come for me."

"Mallory, I don't have a driver," Brad said.

Mallory looked toward Mrs. Rollins standing in the doorway. The housekeeper looked toward Brad, and slowly moved her head from side to side. Mallory's gaze went from Mrs. Rollins to the detectives, who had made eye contact. "What is it? What aren't you telling me?"

"Ms. McGill," Detective Rothman held up a set of keys. "Are these yours?"

"Yes, those are my car keys. But I don't understand."

"We found your car near the creek."

"My car? That can't be."

Cardello flipped back through her pad. "A yellow VW. License plate says LOVMYART." Mallory nodded.

"It's been impounded. Being dusted for prints as we speak."

"But how, why? I didn't drive. How did my car get there? Wait, that's the spare set I keep at Brad's."

Mrs. Rollins sighed. She came into the room and put her arm around Mallory. "Detectives, can't you see the child's upset. Is this all necessary?"

"I'm afraid it is." Detective Cardello cleared her throat. "Ms. McGill, I understand that you are self-supporting."

"Yes."

"Exactly how do you earn your livelihood?"

"I paint. I paint portraits. And I get commissions to do murals."

"Murals?"

"Paintings on large buildings."

"I know what murals are. How do you get these commissions?"

"Detective Cardello," Brad said, taking Mallory's hand in his, "what has this got to do with Ms. McGill's baby?"

Cardello held up a hand. "If you please… Ms. McGill, my question? The commissions?"

"One of my murals had been featured in the Sunday section of the *New York Times*, along with an article about me. I've been getting calls from across the country ever since. That was how I met Keith."

"Keith?"

Mallory's lower lip began to tremble. "My baby's father," she whispered.

Brad came to her side. "They were going to be married."

"No, we were ma…" Mallory heaved a sigh. "It doesn't matter any more. Nothing matters… except my baby."

Mallory's unfinished sentence hadn't gone unnoticed by Cardello. She noted the word "reluctance" on her pad, but said nothing.

"So I take it you travel, Ms. McGill," Detective Rothman asked.

"For my work, occasionally I do."

"It sounds to me like you love the work you do."

"Yes. Very much."

"So a baby would hamper all of that freedom, that traveling?" Cardello said.

"No. Absolutely not," Mallory jumped up from the chair. "I don't have to travel. I had enough job requests in the New York area to support both me and my baby for a long time. Oh God, I want my baby, my little girl," Mallory collapsed back into the chair. "Her room was all ready for her. Her furniture was there and everything."

She turned to Brad. "Brad, you tell them. You saw the sweater I was knitting."

"Mallory, I saw you knitting."

"The walls were covered with painted nursery rhyme characters. Old Mother Hubbard, the Three Little Kittens. Above the window I'd painted The Cow Jumping Over the Moon, so she could see it from her cradle. And her layette was all ready with little nighties, shirts, booties. The tiny sweater I'd made to bring her home from the hospital in. There was a beautiful little teddy bear, and the Jack-in-the-Box. I'd found one just like I had when I was a child. It was square, with a small crank and a red knob that you wound. It played 'Pop Goes the Weasel.'"

Mallory, forgetting the others were in the room, hugged her belly and rocked back and forth. In a trance-like state, she sang softly. "All around the mulberry bush / The monkey chased the weasel / The monkey thought 'twas all in fun / Pop goes the weasel."

"Thank you, Ms. McGill."

"Pop goes the weasel. Pop goes the weasel. Pop goes the…"

"Ms. McGill," Detective Rothman gently took Mallory's limp hand from her lap.

Mallory looked up.

"Do we have your permission to look through your apartment?"

"Yes."

Detective Cardello pulled a form and a pen from her pocket. Rothman took them from her and held them out to Mallory. He said gently, "We'll need your signature giving your consent."

Mallory took the paper and the pen.

"Mallory, I don't think that's a good idea," Brad said.

"I have nothing to hide," she said, and signed the paper without looking it over.

"Thank you, Ms. McGill. We'll call you if we have any more questions, and you have my card… in case you think of something you want to tell us."

Mallory nodded.

"If you'll permit me," Brad walked Cardello and Rothman to the door.

"Detectives," Mallory raised herself to a standing position, "I don't know how my car got to the creek, but I do know that my baby is alive. I can feel it."

"I don't know what to do for her," Brad whispered. "She really believes… It's just been too much, too much. First the baby's father."

"Oh?"

"My brother. Seven months ago. There was a leak in his oven. It was a gas explosion."

"I'm sorry for your loss, Mr. Dawson," Cardello said.

Brad nodded, "Thank you. Any word from the divers yet?"

"We'll let you know when we hear."

"Mallory," Brad said, when he returned to the living room, "tell me about your car. How did it get to the creek? You have to be up front with me if you want me to help you."

"I am being up front, Brad, honest. I don't know."

Brad gave her a disdainful look. "Mrs. Rollins, please see to Ms. McGill."

"Please, Brad. You have to believe me."

"I wanted to believe you. I did believe you—until the police found your car at the creek. Why did you make up that story about a car picking you up?"

"I didn't make it up. I couldn't."

Brad left the room, walked into his office, and slammed the door.

"He doesn't believe me. He thinks I did something terrible to my baby. And now Detective Rothman doesn't believe me, either," Mallory said. "Teri Cardello, she was the only one who didn't try to hide her feelings. She just about told me, 'Mallory, you killed your baby.'"

Mrs. Rollins took Mallory's arm. "Come, child," she said.

"I can't blame them, Mrs. Rollins. I'm sure they're wrong, but even if I didn't actually hurt my baby, I let something happen to her. I didn't protect that tiny life I carried. I deserve to die just for that." Breast milk flowed, unchecked, down the front of Mallory's sweater. "What does it matter? What does anything matter now?"

Mrs. Rollins led Mallory back upstairs and to the bedroom. Mallory hesitated on the threshold. "I can't sit in this room and wait. I'll go crazy. I have to do something."

"What? What can you do? The detectives are handling this."

Her anxiety growing, she walked back and forth. "There must be something. She needs me. My baby needs me."

The housekeeper pulled the pill bottle out of her pocket. "Here, take one of these. It will calm you down."

"Calm me down," Mallory screamed. "My baby is missing and you want to calm me down?"

"The police are doing everything they can." She handed Mallory a pill and a glass of water from the night table. "Please."

"You keep giving me pills. Pills won't fix anything. I'm not taking any more." Mallory shoved Mrs. Rollins' hand away. The water glass and the pill went flying.

The housekeeper went into the bathroom, and returned with another glass of water and another pill. "Please. I don't want any trouble with Mr. B," she whispered. "I could lose my job. I'm too old to find other employment. I have nowhere else to go."

Mallory, her eyes on Mrs. Rollins, took the pill. But she held it under her tongue while she swallowed the water.

"Child," Mrs. Rollins said gently, "I'm only following Mr. B's orders. He said he wants you to stay in this room." She closed the door and locked it from the outside.

Mallory spit the pill into her hand. She threw it across the room and sat on the edge of the bed. She had to think. No one believed her, but she *did* hear the crying. She did. She knew her baby was alive.

She paced the floor until she was weak with exhaustion, then sat on the edge of the bed and turned on the television. "*We take you live to Coney Island. More on the young man who was found dead in an alley off Surf Avenue… Authorities believe…*" Mallory was just about to click off the television when the background noises caught her attention. She turned up the volume. The shrieking and laughing and loud music playing were familiar to her. Why? What did it mean? She couldn't remember exactly what, but those noises had something to do with that night. She was sure. She knew she had to get to Coney Island.

She checked the bedroom windows. No fire escapes, no trees to climb down. She went to the door and studied the key hole. Luckily, the house was old, and the door had a lock that could be accessed from either side with a skeleton key. Mallory searched through the desk until she found a large paper clip and a piece of writing paper. She slid the paper under the door. Then straightened the clip and pushed it into the key hole. A slight jiggle and the key on the other side popped out and fell onto the sheet of paper. Carefully, she pulled the paper with the key on it back under the door. She arranged the bed covers so that it looked like she was asleep, then unlocked the door from the inside, taking care to replace the key on the outside of the door again.

The window on the landing overlooked the side of the house and the driveway. She drew back the curtain. Brad's car was just pulling away, but Keith's black Toyota was at the rear of the driveway. Mallory made her way quietly down the stairs. She could hear Mrs. Rollins clattering pots and pans and humming in the kitchen.

The door to Brad's office was open slightly. She slipped in, then repositioned the door as it had been. It was in this masculine room, with its dark paneled walls, that she had met Keith's grandfather, his brother

Brad, and Ruth Rollins, the housekeeper, for the first time. Keith had told her that he and Brad referred to their grandpa as The Grandfather. She'd laughed. Had that been only eight months ago? She stopped for an instant, recalling that fleeting memory from the past as she'd held onto Keith's hand and gone timidly into the den. When she saw the stately old man seated on his tapestry-covered chair, she too began to refer to him as The Grandfather.

"Grandfather, this is Mallory," Keith had said, pride in his voice.

The old Mr. Dawson, squinting, had leaned toward her. "A painter, you said?"

"Yes, Grandfather. And I'm in love with her." Keith's arm protectively encircled her waist, as Mallory's heart skipped a beat.

"So that's how it is, is it," the grandfather had said, chomping on what were obviously false teeth.

"Yes, Grandfather," Keith said, standing taller. "That's how it is."

The old man had leaned even closer to Mallory, and stared into her eyes, studying her silently for a minute or two. Mallory stood tall, accepting his scrutiny, her eyes unflinching, she stared back at him. Nodding his head, he said loudly, "I like this girl. She has spunk."

He'd smiled for an instant, but it was long enough for Mallory to catch the twinkle in his eyes, and she found herself enchanted with the old Mr. Dawson.

Back in the present, Mallory turned to look over the office that was now Brad's. Where would he have put Keith's car keys?

The Grandfather's worn, tapestry-covered chair had been replaced with a comfortable leather one. His record collection had been replaced with the latest high-tech sound system. Bookshelves lined the walls and bordered the window seat. The Grandfather's ornate mahogany desk had been replaced with a sleek cherry one. Mallory headed for the desk. Just as she rounded it, the phone rang, and the front door opened.

"Mrs. Rollins," Brad called from the entry hall, "I'll get it. I forgot my notes."

Mallory dropped to the floor and, clutching her swollen breasts, rolled into the space under the desk. From beneath the desk skirt, she watched Brad's cuffed trouser legs and leather loafers enter the room. They came toward the desk. She held her breath. He stopped at the far end and lifted the phone receiver.

"Everything went exactly as we planned it. No. She has no clue.… Right. I'll take care of the loose ends."

She saw his feet coming around the desk, and put her hand over her mouth. The feet stopped just short of the opening, and turned toward the credenza behind the desk. She heard him shuffle through some files on it, and then leave the room. The front door opened and closed, and Brad's car pulled away. Mallory let out her breath and crawled out from under the desk.

"What are you doing in here? Why aren't you sleeping?"

Startled by Mrs. Rollins' presence, Mallory banged her head as she stood up. "Don't try to stop me. I need Keith's car keys."

"No one's allowed in here." The housekeeper's gaze went quickly to the lacquered box on the desk beside the phone, and then back to Mallory. "He'll be furious if he catches you here."

The kitchen timer rang. She looked toward the kitchen, and then toward Mallory. "Oh dear. My cake. I'll be right back as soon as I've taken it out of the oven. Don't disturb anything," Mrs. Rollins said, hurrying off to the kitchen.

Mallory quickly opened the box on the desk. She pawed through a jumble of keys until she recognized the remote for the Toyota.

She grabbed it and hurried out of the house. Once in the car, she drove to Ocean Parkway, then turned left, going the way the driver had taken her. She passed Coney Island Hospital and continued on, acutely aware of how different everything looked in the daylight. Just before the beach, she turned right. That's where the driver had been turning when she'd tried to get his attention. She'd remembered nothing after that.

Mallory drove past the New York Aquarium, past the Cyclone. She heard shrieking and pulled to the side of the street. She closed her eyes, and listened to the sounds again. Yes, she had been here. That was the noise she'd heard on Monday night, too. She remembered. Concentrating on where the other sounds might lead her, she pulled back into traffic. Oblivious to her grumbling stomach and the pain that radiated from her breasts, Mallory drove on, slowly, erratically. She caught the aroma of the hot dogs at Nathan's, and swerved across the double yellow line and back again. A car jammed on its brakes. Tires squealed. A horn blared.

Traffic slowed behind her. A truck driver, cursing loudly, pulled around, into the lane of oncoming traffic. An approaching car turned sharply, avoiding the truck by inches. Mallory stopped short. The car behind her squealed to a stop. More horns blasted. She took a deep breath and rested her head on the steering wheel. Traffic inched around her. Drivers screamed at her in an assortment of languages. Some raised their middle fingers as they drove past her car.

A rapid tapping on her window made her bring her head up swiftly. A young policeman signaled her to roll the window down. "What seems to be the problem, Miss?"

"I… uh… I…"

"You look a little confused. Let me see your license, please."

Unconsciously, Mallory reached for her bag on the seat beside her. Then remembered the circumstances that had brought her here. "I must have left my purse home, officer."

"Pull your car to the side of the road. Then give me your keys, please." Mallory did as she was told. "Wait here," he instructed. He went back to his car to call in her license number.

"Sorry, Miss, but you'll have to come with me," the officer said when he returned.

Wearily, Mallory climbed into the rear of the patrol car. The officer made a U-turn, and after a few short blocks, made a left onto West 8th Street. They drove under the newly renovated elevated subway station. Just past the train line, police officers milled about in front of a concrete building. A sign above the door read 60th Precinct Station.

The officer led Mallory up several steps, and held the door open as she entered the dismal building where several officers in a heated discussion were blocking the front desk. "My Mets will kick your Yankees' butts," one said.

"Oh yeah? Put your money where your mouth is."

"I'm in for five."

"Ten here."

The officer nodded to a chair, and Mallory sat down. She closed her eyes and put her hands over her ears, forcing herself to shut out the voices around her. She had to think. She rocked back and forth, trying to make sense of this thing that made no sense. What was going on?

Detective Rothman came out of the office he and Cardello shared. Seeing Mallory sitting and rocking, he looked questioningly toward the desk sergeant. Lazaro shrugged. "She didn't have a license with her. Seemed kind of spaced out when O'Reilly brought her in."

Detective Cardello walked out of her office carrying a load of files. "I'm up to date and ready for my well-earned—" she stopped mid-sentence when she saw Mallory. "What the f—"

Rothman put his finger to his lips. Cardello shut her mouth and shrugged.

He needn't have bothered. Mallory, deep in thought and unaware of the detectives, continued to rock. *Who would want to take my baby? Why hadn't Brad come to drive me when I went into labor? Why did Mrs. Rollins say I hadn't called? If I didn't, who sent the car for me?*

But the detectives said my car was found at the creek. How could it have gotten there unless I drove it myself? Did I? No. And I did hear the crying. If I had done what they all seemed to think I had, there would have been no crying baby.

And Brad, hearing him when I was hiding under the desk, "She has no clue," he said. "I'll take care of the loose ends." What had he meant? What loose ends? Was I a loose end? Was my child?

"Ms. McGill," Rothman said, quietly patting her hand. "Have you come to see me?"

Mallory looked up, startled. "I'm sorry. I was… thinking." Then, with more strength, "Yes. Detective Rothman, I *would* like to talk to you."

He nodded, waiting.

"I remember some things. Noises, I think…"

Brad walked in just then. "Mallory," he said. She stopped mid-sentence. "I'll take care of her," he said to the detectives without so much as a hello first.

"I couldn't stay at your house. I had to find out."

"I know." He took Mallory's arm and helped her up.

"I was just telling Detective Rothman—"

"It's all right, Mallory. You don't have to tell him anything. Let's go."

The desk sergeant handed Brad the keys to Keith's car. "It's parked on Surf Avenue, Mr. Dawson, across from Nathan's. Traced you from the license plate."

"Thanks. I'll have someone pick it up later."

Rothman and Cardello watched as Brad hustled Mallory out of the door. "She looked confused, bewildered," Rothman said. "But not like the kind of woman who would kill her own baby."

"Ha." Cardello dropped her files on the counter. "She was probably headed back to the scene of her crime. You know what they say, the criminal always returns—"

"I don't think so. It seemed like she was trying to tell us something before that Dawson guy barged in."

"He was in quite a hurry to get her out of here. What do you make of that?"

Rothman shrugged. "He seemed edgy. Just became more than a person of interest in my book."

"Mine, too."

"Brad, you've got to listen to me," Mallory pleaded as Brad, holding her arm, led her out to the car.

"Mallory, I've tried. But you haven't told me anything. I want to help you. You know I care about you. Just tell me the truth, and I'll do everything I can for you." He opened the door, and Mallory sat down.

"I am telling the truth," she said, running her hands through her hair.

"And that is?" He paused at the open door.

"I don't know," Mallory whispered. "That is the truth. I don't know. But you can't keep me from finding my baby."

"Why would you think I'm doing that? I have no clue."

Where had Mallory heard "no clue" before? Brad's phone call. He'd said, "She has no clue."

Brad closed her door and went round to the driver's side.

She moved as far away from him as she could.

He looked over at her. Her thoughts were unreadable but there was no mistaking the anger and resolution written across Mallory's face. "Would you rather I dropped you at your place," he asked her.

"Yes."

Brad turned off Ocean Parkway. He made a right on Avenue N, a left onto East 17th Street, and stopped at the apartment building. The lock clicked open. He waited.

Mallory opened the door and stepped out.

"Take care of yourself, Mallory," he said gently.

"I intend to." *Why was he being so agreeable all of a sudden? What did he have up his sleeve,* she wondered.

"You know you're welcome to come back any time you want to, Mallory. You don't have to go through this alone."

"Thank you," she said stiffly, closing the car door behind her. She made her way slowly through the courtyard, glad to see that Mr. Lowenthal wasn't at his usual place at the window. No need for her to engage in conversation or tiptoe past. The front door had been left ajar, and across the lobby, the out-of-order sign was still pasted on the door of the elevator. So, once again, Mallory trekked up the stairs to her apartment, stopping to catch her breath on each landing. It wasn't until she finally reached the fifth floor and knelt at the radiator that she remembered she didn't have her spare key. Brad had taken it from her, and she had no idea where her purse was. The hall light was out. Exhausted, despondent, she slid to the floor of the dark hall.

Sitting against her door, her back hunched over, her knees drawn to her chin, she pulled her sweater over her legs, wrapped her arms around them, and sobbed. Her sobs echoed in the empty hall. She put her hands over her mouth to silence them. But not before she heard footsteps on the stairs. She held her breath, hoping Brad hadn't come after her again.

Step, step, step, step. Then, thud, thud, thud. And again step, step, step, step, followed by thud, thud, thud.

Relief. That had to be Moses.

Moses took the stairs three at a time then dribbled his ball as he rounded each landing. Mallory couldn't remember ever seeing Moses without that ball.

She thought of the first time she'd watched him. Partially hidden by the shrubs on the perimeter, she had been sketching the basketball court, when he'd come into the yard through the break in the fence. Alone, he dribbled the ball around his back and through his legs. Then he made basket after basket.

She remembered being impressed with his confidence. The Judge certainly was the right nickname for him.

"Ms. McG, is that you?" Mallory didn't answer. Moses flicked on his cigarette lighter and extended it toward her. "Oh, shit. Ms. McG, you look awful. Is this your time? Are you in labor?"

Mallory's sobs turned into anguished cries.

Moses flicked off his lighter. "Stay where you are. I'll be right back." He ran down a flight of stairs and pilfered a bulb from the fourth floor landing. Seconds later, he returned and screwed it into the wall fixture, bathing Mallory in a dim yellow light. Moses reached out to touch her head. Then, hesitant, he pulled his hands back and dropped down to his knees on the cold tile floor instead.

A nearby door opened a crack. "You touch one hair on that woman's head and I'll clobber you." The door closed, and Mallory could hear the chain sliding open. Then the door opened wide and the little, bell-shaped woman clad in a flowered house dress and black rain boots stepped into the hall brandishing a big umbrella. Grey hair, wet and stringy, hung down one side of her head. The other side of her head was covered with large pink rollers. One roller slowly unwound and bounced on the floor. Despite her anguish, at the sight of her elderly neighbor, Mallory's lips curled into a tight smile.

"Mrs. Russo, it's all right. Really. Please go back inside. Moses is my friend."

Moses picked up the renegade roller and held it up to the lady, like a peace offering.

"What's this," she asked, examining the roller as though she'd never seen it before.

"It's your roller, Mrs. Russo. You were setting your hair," Mallory said.

She touched her wet head. "Oh, yes, thank you dear."

"Now please go inside. It's all right."

"Well, okay. But you holler if you need me. Y'hear?" The old woman took the roller and returned to her apartment. She slid the chain back into place.

Using the back of her hand as a tissue, Mallory wiped the tears from her face. "Poor lady, she's becoming so forgetful." Then she patted the floor next to her. Moses moved to her side.

"Ms. McG, what's happening? What can I do? Ms. McG?"

"I'm sorry, Moses, I was… never mind."

"I got to worrying about you. Haven't seen you working on the mural since last Sunday. And you weren't home on Monday night when I stopped by."

Mallory's reply was a deep sigh.

"Ms. McG, you OK? Anyone mess with you, you just tell me. I'll take care of them."

"Thank you, Moses, it's that… Oh Moses, I lost the baby."

"Oh shit—uh, sorry Ms. McG—I mean… damn. That's tough."

"I can't remember much of it. It was all so weird. Like I was having a nightmare, being dragged down a narrow alley. I woke up in a hospital. Detectives kept asking me what I did with my baby."

"Detectives?"

"They said they found me at Coney Island Creek."

"I'll check around. I know them dudes that hang out at that creek. Crackheads, scum. See what I can find out. But I can't leave you sitting here like this."

"The Super has an extra key to my apartment. Can you get it for me?"

"Ms. McG, just look at you. You shouldn't be staying on the fifth floor with no elevator."

Mallory leaned her head back against the wall and sighed. "You're right. The stairs almost did me in. I have to save my energy to find my baby."

"You can stay with me and my brother Marcus until your elevator is working."

"No. I think I should go back to Brad's. When he picked me up from the hospital and brought me to his house… well, there was something he wasn't telling me. If he had some connection with my baby's disappearance, I should be close by to figure out what."

"Yeah, like, 'Stay close to your friends, but stay closer to your enemies.'" Moses stood up and held a hand out to help Mallory up. "Maybe going back there does makes sense. But you be careful."

Chapter 15

Mrs. Rollins had just placed the standing rib roast into the oven for Thursday's dinner when the phone rang. "May I speak to Brad, it's Charlotte Assanato."

"Charlotte. What a nice surprise. How are you? What has it been? Ten years, fifteen? You know Mr. B still talks about you. He says he never had a better secretary. I'm sure if you ever want to come back to work for him, you just have to say the word."

"No, Mrs. Rollins. I don't think so. That was lifetimes ago. Before my marriage. Before my little boy… died."

"Yes. What a terrible tragedy. And your poor brother. Tell me. How is he doing? Frank, wasn't it? I hope he's kept his nose clean since Mr. B got his conviction overturned."

"He's done so well. Hasn't touched a drop of alcohol, went back to school. He's working as a paramedic now. But I need to talk to Brad. The last few months Frank's been very angry and frightened. I'm worried about him. He used to confide in me, but now he won't tell me anything. Sometimes he won't even answer his phone. Brad was so kind to him, taking on his case and all—I suggested that Frank call him, but he blew up and said some really nasty things about him."

"That's strange. I wonder why."

"And then Tuesday, I told him we were rejected by another adoption agency. I was pretty upset. He said not to worry. He said his girlfriend had died and he was going to bring me her baby."

"That was too bad—about his girlfriend dying. But Charlotte, I'm so happy for you."

"No, Mrs. Rollins, it's not like that. Frank never had a girlfriend, or a baby. I think he's going to do something wrong."

"You were right to call. I'll tell Mr. B, and he'll have a nice talk with your brother. Now where can he find Frank?"

"I don't know. He just moved. He wouldn't even tell me where to. And he has a new phone number."

"Well then Charlotte, honey, just give me his number. He surely wouldn't mind that. You do want Mr. B to speak to him."

"Well, yes."

Moses walked Mallory back to Brad's. He watched from the curb, impatiently drumming his fingers on a tree, as she made her way up the path to the front door of the house. What he hadn't told her was what he'd found in a plastic bag in a dumpster—two bloodied sheets with something that looked like the afterbirth his dog had after her puppies were born. That was Wednesday night, two nights after Mallory lost her baby. A coincidence?

Mallory stood on the front step, shifting her weight from one leg to the other. Then, with a deep sigh, she rang the bell. Brad opened the door. Mallory didn't even notice the delicious aroma of Mrs. Rollins' rib roast wafting through the air as it cooked. She shrugged. "The elevator at my place isn't working. I'd, uh, like to reconsider your offer, and stay here."

Brad stepped aside. "Of course. Come in, Mallory."

Although countless polishings had made the dining room table glass-like, Mrs. Rollins continued to polish it daily. She was doing that when she heard Mallory's voice. She stuck the dust cloth in her apron pocket and hurried from the dining room and into the hall. "I'm so glad you're back. Come with me, child," she said. "I'll help you up the stairs."

Mallory pulled away from the housekeeper. "No. You're not going to lock me in that room again."

Brad had been sorting his mail on the hall table. He turned back to the women. "Mallory, what are you talking about?"

"It's nothing, Mr. B. Women stuff. Don't bother yourself about this," Mrs. Rollins said.

"Women stuff?"

She lowered her voice. "The bleeding and all... Ms. McGill should be in bed."

"No. I won't be put to bed like some disobedient child. And I will find my baby."

Brad looked from the housekeeper to Mallory. "Oh, for God's sake. Here are the keys to the house and the car. You can come and go as you please."

"Thank you, Brad."

Mallory took the keys. Her head began to spin, and she slid to the floor. Brad lifted her up and carried her to the club chair near the fireplace in the parlor.

"I told you, Mr. B. This girl needs to rest. And she hasn't eaten and—"

"Please see that she does, Mrs. Rollins."

Mrs. Rollins pulled up the hassock, lifted Mallory's legs onto it, and tucked an afghan around her. "You've got to believe me. I was just doing what was best for you."

Mallory nodded, only half listening to the housekeeper as she watched Brad withdraw into his office. Her thoughts were on the phone conversation she'd overheard earlier as she hid under his desk. Maybe she'd never known him as she thought she did.

"Mrs. Rollins, what can you tell me about Brad?"

"What do you want to know?"

"About his childhood. His mother."

Mrs. Rollins pulled a chair over to Mallory's and sat down. "He had a stepmother…"

"What about his real mother? What happened to her?"

"His mother, umm, she left when he was two."

"Keith told me that Brad never got over having been abandoned by her."

The housekeeper rose abruptly, and, her back to Mallory, dusted the edge of the mantle with the skirt of her apron. "Things like that happen."

Chapter 16

Detectives Cardello and Rothman pulled up to the curb in front of Mallory's apartment building just after she and Moses had turned the corner heading for Brad's house. Mr. Lowenthal was in his usual seat near the window. "Could you direct us to the super's apartment," Rothman asked, as Cardello, never without her camera, pulled out her point and shoot and got a few photos of the building.

"Detectives?" Lowenthal responded, without looking their way.

Rothman waved his hand in front of the man. "Excuse me, sir. Are you... blind?"

Lowenthal chuckled. "Sometimes I forget. Thanks for reminding me."

"How did you know we're detectives," Rothman asked, momentarily sidetracked from the purpose of the visit.

"Handcuffs jingling from your belt. What I can't tell is why you're here." Lowenthal waited expectantly for his curiosity to be appeased.

"The super's apartment?" Cardello reminded him.

"That would be Willie Williams. First floor right side. One D. Knock loud. He's got a mess of kids in there." Lowenthal leaned toward their voices, "And another one in the cooker."

Cardello and Rothman headed down the hall, passing one apartment after another. English, Spanish, and Island dialects blended like music in their ears and smells of chicken soup, meat sauce, ox tail, and curry permeated the air before they reached the super's apartment at the end of the hallway.

Children's laughter echoed behind that door. As they buzzed the bell for the third time, a short, T-shirted, hairy chested man—with a toddler in one arm and a small boy clinging to his leg—opened the door. Cardello flashed her badge. "Are you the super?"

"Yes," came his answer, actually more of a question.

"We'd like to see Ms. McGill's apartment."

"I don't know if..."

"Now," Rothman pulled out the official-looking form Mallory had signed.

"Sure, sure." Turning his head from them, he hollered into the apartment, "Joanna, come get these darn kids." He shrugged apologetically, feigning annoyance with his children, but nuzzled the neck of the little one in his arms. The child giggled.

A short, rosy-cheeked woman appeared behind him. Two dark, curly heads peered out from behind her. The oldest, who couldn't be more than five or six, squeezed past. "Going outside, Mama."

"You stay in the courtyard, Thomas. You hear me?" She collected the toddler from her husband's arms, and took the other child by the hand. The super patted his wife on the rear as she herded her brood back into the apartment.

"Later, baby."

She looked over her shoulder at him, lowered her eyes, and smiled shyly.

Willie Williams grabbed his key ring off a hook near the door and led Cardello and Rothman up the stairs.

"What kind of tenant is Ms. McGill," Rothman asked.

"She's a good tenant. Minds her own business. What is it you're looking for?"

The super's question was met with silence.

After several minutes of searching through his key ring, Willie opened the door to 5B.

Cardello stepped into the small foyer and pulled Rothman in. "Thank you for your help," she said, closing the door before Willie could join them.

From previous cases, they could draw the layouts of these basic mirror-image apartments. They stood in the foyer now—just large enough for a small round table and two chairs. On their right, a tiny kitchen with a pass-through beside the doorway opened to the foyer/dining area. Straight ahead, even with the shades drawn, enough light came through the windows at the opposite end of the large open room for them to be able to see a futon in the middle of the longer wall, and a bureau next to that. Opposite the futon, a rocking chair stood next to a small television on a cheap stand.

Cardello pulled out her camera and snapped away.

While he pulled on his rubber gloves, Rothman walked through to the foyer, turned right, and headed past the kitchen and down the narrow hallway. The first door on the left opened to a closet; the next door opened to a bathroom. On the right, another door opened into a small room. The one window opposite the door faced the air shaft, and even though it was morning, and the shade was up, barely any light found its way into this room. Canvases of various sizes leaned against the walls.

Cardello flicked on the light and squeezed past the three-by-five foot canvas perched on a standing easel in the center of the room. She turned to see the rudimentary painting on it. Paint brushes were strewn carelessly about the small table near the easel. "Nadine paints. She'd have a fit if she ever saw clean brushes laying around like that. And these in the can, bristles-down." She touched a tube of paint. It was beginning to harden. The cap was nowhere around.

Rothman looked down. "The room smells of paint, but there's no sign of any blue paint on the floor here."

"No sign McGill was preparing for a kid, either. About the only part of the fantasy she got right was the pale green walls. She had no plans to bring an infant here. Remember how meticulously Nadine and I prepared the room for our baby?"

"Hope you're wrong, Teri," Rothman said heading back to the large room, where a small area rug in its center seemed totally out of place given the proportion of the room.

"Looks like she sleeps here." Cardello said, taking in the pillow and blanket on the futon.

Rothman went back to the hallway and looked through the shelves in the closet, while Cardello checked through the medicine cabinet in the bathroom. Then, stepping over Brad's shirt and pants that Mallory had dropped when she'd come back to change, she went through the hamper until the ringing telephone drew them both back into the front room.

They waited, and shortly the answering machine on the dresser clicked on. "Ms. McGill, this is Doctor Pusitari. I was just calling to see how you were feeling. You missed your appointment on Monday."

Cardello looked at Rothman, and pointed to the answering machine. "You still think she's telling the truth? Never showed for her check-up."

Rothman shrugged.

Closing the door behind them, they walked down the five flights and into the bright courtyard. The curly headed child who'd rushed past them from the super's, a short time before, was sitting on the step winding the red knobbed crank of a Jack-in-the-Box. "All around the mulberry bush / The monkey chased the weasel / The monkey thought 'twas all in fun…" The child turned the knob more slowly, until the lid popped open and a clown's head on a spring jumped out while the box played "Pop goes the weasel." He squealed delightedly, and stuffed the clown back into the box. Then turned the crank again.

"I know," Rothman said. "That's another part of the fantasy she got right."

"Good bye, detectives," Mr. Lowenthal called from his window.

Chapter 17

After finishing their search of Mallory's apartment, Cardello and Rothman headed to Lincoln High School where a secretary had agreed to meet them and look through the student records, even though it was her vacation time.

Then, with Eduardo Gonzalez's address in hand, they headed toward Elgart Street, passing housing projects, occasional clusters of smaller ramshackle houses, and empty lots filled with debris. On some, small urban farms flourished amidst the rubble. Liquor stores, welfare offices, and methadone clinics burgeoned in this area.

Meanwhile, Thompson paced the floor in his apartment. He checked his watch. 3:00 P.M. He'd been checking his watch for most of the day. The infant was small but breathing well, for the present. He'd gotten some formula into him, and changed his diaper. He'd purchased a couple of baby gowns, preemie sized, and receiving blankets on Brighton Beach Avenue, before he'd coaxed Dora into his apartment to take her baby. Wouldn't do to have his delivery stamped "Coney Island Hospital." The infant lay wrapped in the blanket and ready to be put into the gym bag. The exchange was set for 3:30. That would be none-too-soon to get this off his hands. With the wad of bills he'd be getting for this transaction, in addition to what he'd been stashing away, he'd have enough to get him settled into a new life. His bags were packed, and he'd booked his flight to Alaska. The earliest one he could get. Friday afternoon. One more day and he would be on his way to a new life.

At 3:15, he put the baby into the gym bag, and put two small bottles of formula in with it. It was a snug fit, but newborns were used to being confined. Slipping the strap over his shoulder, and cradling the half-zipped bag with one arm, he locked his door behind him.

Just as he stepped out of the alley, a black car pulled to the curb behind his old Ford. A man and a woman jumped out and flashed their badges. Thompson looked around, with an expression like that of a cornered animal who knows there's no escape. He clutched the bag to him. His face paled, and he stopped.

"I'm Detective Cardello. We have some questions for you."

He waited, barely breathing. To have come so close....

"We're looking for the landlord."

"That would be me," Thompson said, the word "me" catching in his throat.

"Do you have a tenant by the name of Eduardo Gonzalez?"

Thompson's body relaxed slightly.

"Uh, sure. He rents a room here."

The kid, a drugged-out teenager who lived on the top floor, had been the one thing that had almost stopped Thompson from buying the place. But there wasn't much else in his price range and in an area where his business would be ignored.

"We need to see his place."

Thompson looked at his watch. "I have an appointment…"

Cardello pulled out a folded piece of paper. "I have a warrant."

"Can't you come back some other time?" Thompson zipped the gym bag, taking care to leave a couple of inches open. He held it closer. "Look, I was just leaving for the gym. Can't this wait?"

"No. But it shouldn't take long."

"I, uh… I have to get the key. I'll be right back."

Cardello watched as Thompson walked back down the alley, and very carefully lowered the bag to the step before unlocking the door. A moment later, he emerged from the apartment and relocked all three deadbolts, before hurrying back to the detectives—without his bag. He took the steps up to the front porch two at a time, Cardello and Rothman right behind. "That where you live," Rothman asked, nodding toward the boarded-up windows that faced the porch.

"I'm a mechanic. I keep my tools here. In this neighborhood—well, I don't have to tell you how it is." Quickly, he unlocked the front door. "I'm planning to get gates and an alarm system."

Once Mallory was back at Brad's house, Moses returned to Eduardo's place to shadow that guy who'd come out of the ground-floor apartment. If what he'd found in the dumpster had anything to do with Mallory, he couldn't wait. He made his way through the neighboring yards into

Eduardo's, and checked the alley toward the rear of the house. No. The side door was out of the question, with the deadbolt locks firmly in place. And the windows were boarded up. There was always the front door, but that was too risky. Someone might see him. So he climbed the fire escape, and once again crawled through Eduardo's window.

Making his way over the rubble in the apartment, Moses reached the door that led to the hall. He listened. No sound. He tiptoed down one flight of stairs and tried the two doors on the second-floor landing. One was locked, but the knob turned when he tried the second. He let himself into the empty place. Broken pipes jutted from the wall and floor where the sink and toilet had been. "Eduardo, you dog. More of your handiwork? How many times did I tell you, never piss where you sleep, you dumb fuck.… Oh well, it doesn't matter now."

Moses left the vandalized apartment, stepping into the hallway just as the front door opened and voices sounded downstairs. He stepped back in and put his ear to the door.

"Anyone else rent here?" The no-nonsense-woman's voice floated up the stairs.

Moses recognized it as the basketball-playing detective who had questioned him about Eduardo.

"Uh, no." Thompson hurried up the stairs, past the two closed doors on the second landing.

"Empty," he said, catching Rothman's look.

Without pausing, Thompson continued on to the third floor. He tried a key, but the door opened before he turned it.

"The kid must have left it unlocked."

Cardello scrunched her nose. Rothman let out a low whistle.

"Not tidy, but he didn't give me any trouble," Thompson said.

"Wait here," Cardello instructed him as she and Rothman pulled on their gloves. Thompson, standing in the doorway, shifted from one foot to the other. He checked his watch as the detectives methodically went through each pile of clothes on the floor, pocket by pocket. Next, the detectives turned over the coffee can and emptied the grinds, and then did the same with the take-out containers scattered about the floor. Thompson checked his watch again as they shook out the sheets from the bed, and felt around the molding above the door and the window. Sweat ran down his armpits.

"Nothing here." Rothman finally announced.

"Clean here, too. Do you know if he had any family?"

"No ma'am. He said he had no one."

"What a crock of shit. He had a mother and a sister," Moses mumbled from the doorway below.

Thompson closed the door behind them as soon as they stepped out of the apartment.

Rothman paused. "What's the smell in here?"

"Disinfectant. I clean the hall with it," Thompson answered as he headed downstairs.

"In a hurry," Rothman asked.

"I told you, I have an appointment."

Once they reached the street, Cardello put out her hand. "Thank you for your help." Thompson nervously shook it.

"We'll be in touch if we have any more questions," she said.

Moses tiptoed out of the vacant apartment, and closed the door quietly behind him. He ran his hand over the molding. "He cleaned this hall, my ass. That disinfectant smell's coming from the boarded-up apartment." He exited the way he had come in—through Eduardo's apartment and down the fire escape.

As soon as the detectives were back in their car, Thompson looked at his watch again. 3:35. He ran back to his apartment.

As she neared the corner, Cardello glanced in her rearview mirror. Thompson, carefully carrying the gym bag, was walking at a fast clip in the opposite direction, and he was almost to Surf Avenue.

"That landlord sure was nervous, and I never saw someone in such a big hurry to get to a gym. Especially a guy as thin as he is," Rothman said, patting his own gut. "I'm the one who should be going."

"There's something strange about that man, but I just can't put my finger on it."

Rothman turned to see what his partner was looking at. Just then, Moses came out of the alley and hurried after Thompson. "Isn't that the kid from the school yard, who said he didn't know where Eduardo lived?"

Cardello put the car into reverse, backed up, gave it gas, and made a quick U-turn. Dodging traffic on the one-way street, she and Rothman pulled up to Surf Avenue just as Thompson crossed the street with Moses on his tail.

Rothman adjusted his holster, " Let's see what this is all about." He opened the car door and started off after Thompson and Moses. Cardello was cruising slowly beside him when a 10-24 came in. Officer down. That took precedence. Rothman jumped back into the car as she floored the pedal and, siren blaring, shot out into traffic.

Moses' passion was detective work. Requiring little sleep, he watched all of the *CSI* shows and all of the *Law & Order* shows On Demand in the early morning hours. Now he followed Thompson as the man crossed Surf Avenue and turned right, headed toward the empty MCU Park. He'd been there many times with his brother, Marcus, to watch the Cyclones play.

While this end of Coney Island didn't attract as many beach goers as the area near Stillwell Avenue did, there were enough people on the street for Moses to follow Thompson unnoticed—until Thompson reached the boardwalk.

Having no cover to hide behind on the boardwalk didn't deter Moses. He knew how to tail a guy from a safe distance, and he also knew that making yourself visible made you more invisible. His brother had taught him that.

Thompson sat down on a bench across from the old red, yellow, and blue, parachute jump. He placed his gym bag carefully on the seat beside him, and opened it a bit. He looked at his watch. He tapped his foot on the ground: up and down, up and down. Faster and faster. He looked at his watch again. He stood up, holding the bag by the strap. He patted it. He looked up and down the boardwalk. Bicyclists wove in and out around couples strolling by. Children hurried to the water fountain and back to the beach with pails of water and water guns. A woman, sitting on the beach near the boardwalk, screamed at her kids not to throw sand. And near her, a guy took in the sun, his boom box blasting a loud and obnoxious rap song.

Moses had staggered up the ramp like a drunk, and had flopped on his back on the nearest bench; one leg hanging off, the other bent at the knee, his head lolling to the side. In full view, squinting, he lay on the bench, and watched his mark.

Several more minutes passed before a stocky man carrying a large paper sack of Nathan's fries sat down on the bench Thompson had vacated. Thompson returned to the bench, putting his gym bag gingerly on the boardwalk between his legs. The man reached out and offered him the fries.

Thompson ate one, then threw another toward the beach. The seagulls swooped in, cawing at one another, and fighting over the food. He pulled four or five more out, and threw them to the gulls. As they fought over them, he looked into the greasy food sack the man held, and nodded. Then he lifted the gym bag to the seat between them. He unzipped it and tipped it toward the stocky man. The man looked in. He handed Thompson the fries bag. Thompson rezipped the gym bag part way. The courier carefully lifted it, and took off in the direction of Sea Gate. Thompson stuck the Nathan's bag in the pocket of his sweat shirt, and headed back in the opposite direction.

Moses followed the heavyset man. He turned on 24th Street and got into a green Honda. License number BAR 1723. Moses called his cousin, who worked at the Motor Vehicle Bureau.

As the courier walked off with the infant in the bag, Thompson breathed a sigh of relief. He headed back to his apartment with a new spring to his step. Once inside, he pulled out the crumpled bag he'd stuffed into his pocket and removed the bills. He took a large envelope from the counter, slipped them in, and sealed it. With a kitchen knife, he pried off a floor board and removed a packet of envelopes similar to the one he had just put the bills into. He banded all of the envelopes together. Then he pulled his luggage out from under the his cot.

Chapter 18

"Hi, Rachel," Rothman called, entering the shop as Rachel poured coffee for a young woman. "Sure could use a cup of that myself. It's been one long day."

"You got it, Sam."

"And give me one to go, please. Teri's going to swing around this way and pick me up." He leaned forward to study the pastries in the glass-covered cake stand.

"Come over here. I want you to meet Angie, the girl I've been telling you about. Angie's a nurse."

Angie turned, and she and Rothman laughed.

"So this is *that* Sam. Rachel, we've known each other since elementary school. I love him to bits, but trust me, there's no physical chemistry."

"All right. But," Rachel put a Boston Creme doughnut down in front of Rothman. He looked up, surprised.

"It's Thursday, Sam. That's what you were going to choose after you studied all of the pastries. Trust me." She picked up her knitting and began ripping her stitches. "Now you two listen up. S-E-X," she spelled out the letters, "isn't everything…"

"What are you knitting?" Angie asked, changing the subject.

"My landlord and his wife are adopting a baby."

"Aren't they like… old," Rothman asked.

"They're in their late fifties, but that doesn't matter. When you have money, you can buy anything, including babies."

Angie put down her coffee. "Speaking of babies, something disturbing happened in the hospital this morning. A man brought his daughter into the emergency room. She had passed out and was bleeding. Down there." Angie pointed toward her crotch.

"She was a huge girl, mentally handicapped. The father said she was eighteen. Dr. Pusitari examined her, and could tell she'd very recently given birth, but he couldn't get any information from her. The father looked bewildered when the doctor asked him what he knew about the baby—would you believe he didn't know his own daughter was pregnant?

"Dr. Pusitari was so disgusted with the father of the girl that he walked out.

"I asked the man where the baby was. He hesitated for a second or two, like he had to think of an answer before he said, 'my old lady's watching it.'

"I could tell he was lying. I just know something happened to that baby. I could feel it. I called Child Welfare right after they left."

"That could take forever. Angie, get me their address. Off the record. I'll look into it for you."

"That would be great. Thanks, Sam."

Chapter 19

Cardello and Rothman were heading toward the creek to see if they could find out anything new on the McGill case when Angie's call came in.

"Elgart? Between Surf and Mermaid? Are you sure, Angie?"

"I have the girl's file right in front of me."

"Thanks. We'll check it out."

"Surf and Mermaid? Sam that's the same street that—"

"—that Eduardo Gonzalez lived on." Rothman finished her sentence.

The address Angie had given was right next door to the one they had been to earlier that day, in the row of attached houses. But none of the windows in this house were boarded up. "You're certain this is it," Cardello asked, as she pulled to the curb.

"This is the address Angie gave me."

Two kids, maybe ten or twelve, were on the porch, looking in the window, making obscene gestures, and laughing.

"Hey you kids, beat it." Rothman said from the car.

The kids turned at the sound of his voice. "Aw, man. We got a right to look," the taller one said.

"Yeah. Lookin's free," the smaller one added.

A boy on a skateboard zipped across the street, jumped the curb, and grabbed the board as it flew from under his feet. "Hey, Marco, they be havin' a matinee inside?"

"It's Thursday, ain't it? He bees doin' the dirty."

"Do any of you live here," Detective Cardello asked.

"Nah. Just Dora and her old man."

"What about his wife, her mother?"

"She be dead."

The boy turned back to the window as Rothman got out of the car. "Shit, he really hurtin' her this time. Look at all that blood."

Rothman jumped the steps and pushed the kid away, taking his place at the window. "That's *Dora* and her father?"

"Yeah."

"Oh Christ." Rothman brought up his knee and kicked the door open. Splinters flew from the old wood frame. The man, looking angry, scrambled off the girl. He pulled a pair of red suspenders up over his hairy arms, bringing his pants from his knees to below his pot belly, just as Rothman grabbed him by his grungy T-shirt.

"What the hell do you want? Barging in here. Bothering a man on his day off?"

"I'll do more than that, you filthy piece of slime. Is anyone else here?" Rothman asked, shaking him. "Answer me, you fucking prick."

"No, no. Just me and my girl, there."

Rothman slammed him into the door frame. Then he shoved him to the floor.

"Please, take it easy," the man pleaded.

"Take it easy? Girl just has a baby and her old man's fucking her brains out. You probably knocked her up too, you fucking animal."

"I don't know what you're talking about." The man, cowering on the floor, pushed his long thinning hair back from his pock-marked, unshaven face.

Cardello pulled her gun out and checked the other rooms. "Clear." She headed upstairs, her gun still drawn. "Clear," she called on her way back down. She picked up an afghan from the floor, and covered the massive girl, who was naked from the waist down. She helped her to a sitting position on the couch. "Honey, where is your baby? Can you tell me?"

Dora pulled a rag doll out from where it was squished into the corner of the couch. "Dora's baby. Nice baby." She picked up a ragged piece of embroidered cloth and put it on the doll. "Pretty." Then she held it up to Cardello. "Dora give you pretty."

"Thank you, sweetheart." The detective stuck the rag into her pocket, and pulled out her cell phone.

"Her mother used to—"

"Don't open your fucking mouth. You're under arrest. You have the right to remain silent..." Rothman said.

"Child Protective Services," Cardello said into the phone, as Rothman cuffed the man.

*   *   *

"Teri, give me the keys. I need to drive." Rothman said after they'd made their arrest and finished their report at the precinct. He slammed the door behind him and sat for a minute, his hands on the steering wheel and his head resting on his hands. "I swear I was ready to kill that bastard."

"I know how you feel, Sam. I could have castrated him myself."

"Well, he won't be touching anyone else for a long, long time." Rothman pulled away from the curb and turned west on Mermaid Avenue.

"Sam, you're not headed for the creek again. The uniforms have been over that area with a fine tooth comb."

"I just want to take a walk. After that business with that scumbag, I need to breathe some clean air."

"Here? At this dumping ground?"

Rothman shrugged. Cardello sighed, but she zipped her jacket and got in step with him as he headed across the dried grass toward the shoreline.

On one of the benches along the service road, two old women sat, taking in the late summer sun, while an old man fished from the sea wall at the water's edge. To their left, near a narrow, sandy strip of land, ripples bounced off the wreckage of a row boat submerged in the mud.

Beyond that, further down the creek side, yellow ribbons fluttered in the breeze. Crime tapes with their warnings DO NOT CROSS were commonplace in this crime-infested neighborhood. And children played tag near the cordoned-off area. Inside their perimeter, police stood, watching as a diver surfaced, then submerged again.

Cardello sighed. "Elsewhere, yellow ribbons mean hope. Tying off crime scenes, the same color means hope is gone." She turned to the sergeant standing nearby. "Anything yet?"

"Nah. They'll keep at it as long as daylight lasts, but between you and me, if it was down there, it's crab food now."

"No," Mallory cried out from the tall beach grass where she'd been sitting unnoticed on the other side of the police line. "Don't say that. You don't know."

The detectives and the police turned toward the voice.

"What are you doing here, Ms. McGill," Rothman asked, parting the grass to better see the girl who looked more like a lost waif than a woman under investigation for the disappearance of her baby.

"I had to see where they said… you know."

Rothman kneeled in front of her. "You shouldn't be here. Come on. I'll take you home."

Mallory stumbled as she tried to get up, and fell back to the ground. Then she took the hand that Rothman offered.

"I... uh... I'm just a little wobbly."

"When's the last time you ate?"

"I don't remember."

"Come on. I know a good diner. Teri?"

Cardello shrugged. "I can use a good walk. I'll hitch a ride back to the precinct with the sergeant later."

The Parkview Diner on Cropsey Avenue had a clientele that mirrored the city's diverse ethnic population. Waiters and waitresses hurried from table to table taking orders. Busboys were busy carrying bread baskets, and plates of cole slaw, beets, and chick peas to the tables.

"What would you like?"

Mallory shrugged. "I'm not very hungry."

"We'll have hamburgers, fries, and vanilla shakes," Rothman said when the waiter appeared.

Mallory watched the detective eat one pickle and then another while they waited for their meals. When their food arrived, Mallory nibbled at her burger. Rothman covered his in ketchup. He devoured it quickly, and then finished both orders of their fries. "You learn to eat fast in my line of work. Never know when a call's going to come in."

"Detective Rothman, I appreciate the burger, but if this is your way of getting me to talk, you're wasting your time. I can't remember anything other than what I've already told you. You've got to believe me."

Rothman leaned across the table and looked deeply into Mallory's eyes. "I do believe you."

"It doesn't really matter. I didn't kill my baby."

An older couple at the nearest table gasped simultaneously, and turned toward them. Mallory leaned closer to Rothman.

"I could never have done that. But I *let* something happen to her. Don't you understand? I let someone take my baby, so I'm guilty anyway." Mallory rocked back and forth at the table. "I don't care what they do to me, but I need to find her. I know she's alive."

Rothman put down the shake. "Then let me help you. Try to remember. There must be something, anything."

"It's no use. I can't remember."

Across the room, dishes and glasses shattered. A waitress screamed, "She's choking. She's choking!" Everyone looked to see a woman clutching her throat. A man jumped up and grabbed her from behind. His arms locked together under her chest. He lifted her off the ground.

Mallory jumped up, dropping her glass and knocking over her chair. She flung her arms across her chest. Her skirt caught on the arm of the chair. It ripped.

The piece of meat lodged in the woman's throat popped out of her mouth. She coughed. The diners applauded, then went back to the dishes in front of them.

Mallory continued to stand, frozen.

"What is it?" Rothman was standing next to her.

She shook her head. "Something weird. The way he held that woman, with his arms under her chest. I could feel it, like they were tightening above my pregnant belly. I was pulled from the car, dragged into an alley. I opened my eyes. It was pitch black. No lights. I saw the stars in the sky. I cried out, and someone covered my face as a light blinked on."

He uprighted her chair and helped her back into it. "You bruised yourself," Rothman said, nodding toward a purple, strawberry-shaped mark on the outside of her right thigh.

Mallory looked down, and traced the blemish. "A birthmark." A faint smile crossed her lips. "A family trait. My mother had one just like it and so did my grandmother."

Cardello was in no hurry to get back to the precinct. After Rothman left with the McGill girl, she walked along the trampled weed path near Coney Island Creek. In the distance, the low hum of traffic on the Belt Parkway was all that disturbed the otherwise-still air.

The setting sun streaked the sky with brilliant reds and oranges. The sand took on a golden hue. The water gently lapped against the refuse-marred shoreline. Rotting timber, broken loose from long-forgotten barges, half-submerged across the creek, lay in abandonment on the bank near half-buried, rusted shopping carts.

Cardello circled the small sand dunes which flattened out beside the creek, taking care to stay clear of the police markers. The litter-strewn shoreline curved as the creek opened into Gravesend Bay. In the distance, the Verrazano Bridge completed the wide panorama. But Coney Island Creek was less known for its picturesque beauty than for its use as a dumping ground for bodies, most famously by mass-murderer Joel Rifkin in the mid-nineties.

A swirling wind carried a McDonald's sandwich wrapper past Cardello. A Styrofoam coffee cup flew by. Cardello kicked a rusted pot out of her way, and then a piece of an old car muffler.

As she neared Sea Gate, a gated community at the tip of Coney Island, a cat sitting on a log lifted its head and hissed. Its hair stood on end, and it took off as a pack of wild dogs came racing over the rise, growling and tugging at a blue rag as they ran. Cardello stopped short. The dogs stopped, too. They bared their teeth, dropping the rag to the ground. Keeping her eyes on them, she slowly reached down, and even more slowly, picked up a piece of driftwood she'd seen from the corner of her eye. She raised the wood, stepped toward the dogs, and swung it wildly around, screaming all the while. The dogs ran off.

Shaking, Cardello lowered her head and took a deep breath. Then another. With the tip of the wood, she lifted the sand-covered scrap that had landed at her feet. Just as she was about to fling it into the bay, she noticed a bit of pink flesh clinging to it.

She gently lowered it to the ground and took out her camera. She photographed the rag and the bit of flesh attached to it from every angle, and then took some more pictures down the shoreline where the dogs had first appeared. Dialing the station, she said, "I can use an extra body here. We've got to go over this area. Inch by inch." While she waited for backup, she pulled a large paper bag out of her pocket and, with a gloved hand—taking care that the flesh remained with it—lifted the rag into the bag.

Chapter 20

Moses was in the laundromat when he got the call from his cousin, three hours after the guy on the boardwalk walked off with the package.

"Man, what took you so long?"

"You think I sit around the DMV waiting for my dumb-ass cousin to play super spy? I got work to do here."

"Yeah, yeah. What did you find out for me?"

"Moses, I don't know what you got yourself involved in, but if I were you, I'd forget it. Stay clear. The car's registered to an Anthony Dantano."

"Anthony Dantano. Why does that name ring a bell?"

"He's one badass motherfucker. That's why. Now you stay clear of him, or your brother will have my head."

"Don't worry about me. Just checking something out for a friend of mine. What's the address?"

"Howard Beach. No man's land for a black kid. Moses, that's even more reason to stay away. Those fuckers don't fool around."

"I hear you loud and clear. Thanks." Moses pulled the wash out of the dryer before it finished. He stuffed the damp clothes back into the laundry bag, and hightailed it to the library on Mermaid Avenue. He hurried to an empty computer station, and plopped into the seat. He opened Internet Explorer and typed in the name Anthony Dantano.

Sure enough, Dantano's name came up more than a few times. Associated with the mob, fined and jailed for contempt of court—for refusing to answer questions. But he was never convicted of a serious crime. Moses was about to shut the program down when his eye caught the word "baby" under a photograph of a big, burly guy leaving the courthouse. He was flanked by four or five other men. The caption read. "Key Witness Disappears. Dantano Walks Free. Evidence in Baby Selling Operation Inadmissable."

Moses unconsciously emitted a long, low whistle.

The librarian, stacking books on the next table, tapped him on the shoulder and put her finger to her mouth. "Shush."

Moses stopped whistling. "Damn," he said to himself, when she had walked off with the books in a cart. "I almost missed this. I was looking for the guy I saw on the boardwalk." Then he studied the photograph more closely. That guy was one of those in the background. He was the one who had gotten into Dantano's car. Moses printed out the page from the internet, then took it over to the copy machine and enlarged it.

Before he had a chance to think about his next move, Mallory called him. After her dinner with the detective, Rothman had taken her back to her car, which she'd left a block from the creek.

Mallory pulled up, and got out of the car as Moses came out of the library.

"Thanks for coming with me." She handed him the keys. "You drive, and I'll sit in the back. The detectives kept talking about needing something to jar my memory. They asked me if I could remember any smells, sounds out of the ordinary. I've got to try."

At Ocean Parkway and Surf, Moses turned right. He had no choice. Ocean Parkway dead-ended.

"This is where I tried to stop the driver. Keep driving, please." Mallory looked around. "It all happened in the dark. I thought if we could recreate that night…" She held her hands over her eyes, listening intently to the noises as Moses drove past the Cyclone. When he passed Nathan's, Mallory said, "I remember the aroma of hot dogs filled the air that night. The place I was taken to has to be near here."

If only I could separate the real from the imagined, Mallory thought, as Moses drove slowly up and down each street. *An ear in my hand. People cheering for my pain. My car near the creek. My dress torn and bloody.* Mallory turned to better see the left side of the street. It was an effort with the bruises on her rear. *And how did I get those? It has to come together. It just has to.*

On the corner of Surf Avenue, near MCU Park, Moses stopped for a red light. Mallory's eyes were still closed, to simulate the darkness of that night. Loud, excited cheering, whistling, screaming sounds erupted from the stadium. She pinched herself. "I am awake. It can't be the nightmare, this time." She put her hands to her ears to block out the sound. It continued, the same cheering. The noise was real. There was a baseball game going on at MCU Park.

"Yes, I heard that same cheering before, as he was driving me. I'm sure of that. We have to be close."

Moses narrowed their search to the streets within hearing distance of the stadium. Then he drove the same streets again and again.

"Anything seem familiar, Ms. McG?"

Mallory sighed. She opened her eyes. "It's no use. Nothing else is coming to me. Let's go home."

"But it will. You'll remember more and more. You'll see. It will happen." Moses pulled up at an all-night supermarket, and got out of the car with his wash, still damp in its canvas bag. Mallory came around and got into the driver's seat. "I'll keep my phone on," he said, bending his head toward the open window. "You call me anytime, and I'll be there. You hear? We'll find your baby."

"Thank you for believing me, Moses."

"You bet. Now roll up this window, lock your doors, and get home safe. You hear?"

Chapter 21

A short time later Moses came out of the store, the bag with the damp wash over his shoulder, and two plastic bags of groceries dangling from his hand. He turned the corner at the rooming house where he lived with his older brother. Moses did the laundry, the food shopping, and some of the cooking. But Marcus did most of the cooking. Marcus had been paralyzed falling from a skylight while breaking into a house. It had taken him years to learn to walk again.

It was after his brother got hurt that Moses decided he wasn't going to follow that same route. He wasn't going to end up a cripple like his brother. No. He'd use his smarts to get ahead. He'd either get a basketball scholarship or an academic one.

Still, he had to hand it to his brother. He had learned to use the system. He found all the loopholes. He got his hospital bills paid for, he got to go to college for free—Medgar Evers College—on some kind of special program for the handicapped—and he got a top-of-the-line motorized wheelchair when he needed one. In addition, some do-good group that felt sorry for the poor black boy in the chair donated a customized van, so he didn't have to depend on Access-a-Ride to get around.

Now he was being paid to speak at schools to tell kids what happened to him because he tried to rob a house.

As Moses headed home, he studied the license plates on the cars at the curb. Memorizing plate numbers sharpened his memory, and most of these he recognized from the neighborhood. He could look at the numbers and tell who they belonged to without even looking at the makes of the cars themselves. Today he saw a new plate, EJS 1270, and another, BEX 4316. That one was familiar, but from where?

"My mind is like a computer," he said out loud, as he cooked up a pot of pasta. "The answer will come to me." He added the meat sauce he'd picked up at the grocery. Marcus had made a rice pudding, and they had that with ice cream for dessert.

Over dinner, Marcus listened as Moses told him about Ms. McGill and the detectives, and then about the man he'd seen throwing away something that looked like an afterbirth. Then, from his pocket, Moses pulled the copy of the photograph he'd made at the library: Dantano on the courthouse steps. "Do you know anything about this guy?"

His brother took the paper and studied it. "Why do you want to know?"

"Just wondering. I found this photo in the laundromat."

"My ass, you did. Listen up, bro. That guy's a mean mutha. You keep your distance. I'll check around and see what I come up with."

After dinner, Marcus fell asleep in front of their TV. Moses was hanging the damp clothes from a rope he had strung on the fire escape when he heard Vickie singing in her apartment downstairs. "Looking for Paradise" was her favorite song this week.

He picked up his ball and started down the metal fire escape steps to the second floor landing. The lights were on in her room, and her yellow, flowered curtains were open.

Normally, he would have tapped on the window, or called to her if it were open, and she would have invited him in. But she looked so beautiful moving to the Latin beat and singing that he just stood on the platform and watched her. Back and forth she danced, her hips and shoulders gyrating. Never losing her rhythm, she belted out the song as she filled a pitcher with water from the single tap, and emptied it into the tub beside the small refrigerator. She repeated the sequence and the words several times before the tea kettle began to whistle. Taking the pot from the hotplate on top of the refrigerator, she added the steaming water to the tub, refilled it, and put it back on the hotplate.

Still moving with the rhythm of the song, she kicked off her shoes, then unbuttoned her blouse, and slid it off her shoulders. Moses caught his breath. Although he'd seen her naked—she'd deflowered him when he was sixteen—he couldn't take his eyes off her creamy skin against the lace of her black bra.

Spellbound, he lowered himself to a rusted step, and watched Vickie reach behind herself, unclasp her bra, and ease it off. Then she unfastened her skirt, and slid it over her hips and down. Her black thong came off after that, and still her body gyrated. She bent over, twisted her auburn hair, and fastened it on the top of her head with a large hair clamp. The sight of her behind, firm and shapely, made Moses grasp the railing. The kettle whistled again, and she turned to add more steaming water to the tub. He studied her breasts, small and firm, and the triangle of pubic hair between her legs, reddish, like the hair on her head. Still dancing to the rhythm, she hung up her clothes. Then she poured a capful of soap into the tub and swirled the water until bubbles formed.

Gracefully, she stepped into the tub. She lowered her body into the water, sliding down until her face, breasts, and knees, surrounded by soap bubbles, were all Moses could see. Her hands rose from the bubbles and languidly, she caressed her breasts. Then, lifting one leg out of the water, painted toes pointing toward the ceiling, she lathered it with soap. Vickie's back was toward the door, and she didn't see it open, but Moses did. He saw a figure in a navy cap and a tan trench coat tiptoe in, a gun in hand. He froze.

A gloved hand reached over to the dresser and turned off the radio. Vickie turned. She grabbed her towel and scrambled up. "Who are you? What do you want?"

"In good time. All in good time. Now you just sit yourself back down."

Vickie saw the gun as the speaker motioned for her to sit down. Her eyes never leaving the weapon in the gloved hand that pointed at her, she lowered herself back into the tub.

"Now, that wasn't so hard, was it?"

"What do you want? Who are you?"

"Mr. Dawson's associate asked me to stop by. Seems there was a little problem with your friend on Elgart Street."

Moses' ears perked up. "Elgart was where Eduardo lived, and where that man I followed to the boardwalk came from," he whispered to himself.

Vickie held the wet towel tightly to her. "He said we were even. That my debt was clear from when he got me out of jail."

"Well, it seems that the abortionist you referred him to didn't play by the rules…"

"Abortionist? Holy mother of Jesus," Moses whispered. His ball rolled out of his hands. "The gym bag, the guy on the boardwalk, could be Ms. McGill's baby. I've got to get to Howard Beach." He stood up. The platform squeaked. He sat back down.

"I'm a reasonable person," the intruder said. "Just tell me what he did with the baby."

"I don't know about any baby. I haven't spoken to Willard in a long time. You've got to believe me. Please."

"Believe you? A hooker who'd do anything for a buck? Ha. And now the cops are nosing around."

"I wouldn't tell them anything. Honest."

"I know you won't." The figure glanced around, then took a broom from its hook behind the door. "But just to be certain, I have to do a little house cleaning. You do understand." The gloved hand edged the hotplate, still plugged in, closer to the tub.

"No, no. Please!" Vickie's voice filled with terror. Her eyes bulged.

"Tsk, tsk. I tried to be reasonable, to give you another chance, but you had to spoil it by being uncooperative. This is all your fault."

Before Vickie could get out of the tub, the hotplate hit the water. Vickie's mouth opened wide. Her body jerked and twitched. And she was dead. Electrocuted.

Water flew out of the tub. "Oops," the figure said picking up the towel that had fallen onto the floor from Vickie's hand, and wiping the water that had splashed on the coat.

Blotches of suds ran down the yellow walls. Moses put his hand over his mouth to keep from vomiting.

Only after he was certain the killer was gone did he make his way down the rest of the stairs, and throw up behind the rooming house. He lay on the ground, trying to put the pieces together. To understand what had gone down. The address—Eduardo's address—and the bearded guy who dumped the garbage. Something about him being an abortionist. But not doing the abortion.

Vickie had once talked about her friend, Willard someone, who had helped her out when she'd been raped by a John. He'd moved from the rooming house before Moses and Marcus had moved in, but lived somewhere in the area. Could he be that abortionist?

A while later, Moses heard a scream. There was no mistaking the high-pitched voice of old Olivia. Lights came on all over the building. A short time later, sirens sounded. Police cars and an ambulance. He ran through the yard, and jumped the fence. In his neighborhood, cops were prone to take action first and ask questions later. Then Moses remembered the lesson Marcus had taught him, and when he reached the street, he turned toward the entrance of the building and slowed to a walk. If he were visible, he'd be more invisible.

The street was becoming congested with police cars. Moses darted between two, and then jumped out of the way just as Rothman and Cardello pulled up. "Beat it, kid. This is none of your business," Rothman called, getting out of his car. Then he looked more closely. "Aren't you that Moses kid from the basketball court, over at Lincoln High School?"

"Yes, sir, that's me."

"What are you doing here?"

"Officer, sir, I live here. With my brother. Third floor, 3D."

The police car's flashing lights illuminated the building, and the tenants hovering in the doorway. "You just stay out until we tell you you can go in."

"Yes, sir. I surely will." Moses was anxious to check out Dantano, but running off now might look suspicious, so he milled around with the other tenants.

"All right. Who found the body?" Fingers pointed toward Olivia, and Rothman and Cardello forgot about Moses.

An ambulance pulled up, and two paramedics carried their bags into the building.

Chapter 22

Moses walked to the pizza place on the far corner. The same cars that had been parked on the street earlier were still there—all but the one with the BEX 4316 plate on it. Another call to his cousin at the DMV. He'd get the stats on that.

Dirk, his friend, pulled up to the curb. "How's it goin', man?"

"Just made my last delivery. Want to chill," Dirk asked.

"Later, maybe. Right now I need to borrow your car."

"Boss will skin me alive."

"You drive me then." Moses looked into the store. Sal was flipping a pie, his back to the door. "He hasn't seen you yet. Come on. This is important."

Dirk got back behind the wheel as Moses climbed into the passenger side.

"Where to?"

"Head for the Belt, going east."

Moses turned on the radio. Hip hop music blared. They sang along as they drove.

The Belt Parkway was quiet for a summer evening. Almost eerily quiet. Traffic hadn't even bottle-necked where it usually did at exit 15, the Erskine Avenue exit that lead to the Gateway Mall. "Get off at the next exit," Moses said.

"Cross Bay Boulevard? You've got to be shitting me."

"Relax. If anyone asks, we're delivering a pizza."

Dirk went through a light on the Boulevard just as it turned red. Sirens flashed. "Pull over to the side of the road," a speaker blared.

"I'm in big shit. They'll check out my license," Dirk said.

"So?"

"It's a phony. I'm only sixteen."

"That's good. All you'll get is a night at juvie."

"And a beating from my old lady when I get home."

As the police walked toward their car, Moses flipped on the interior lights. "No use agitating these guys."

They sat, Dirk with his hands on the steering wheel and Moses with his on the dashboard, in plain sight, nothing to hide. One policeman went toward the passenger's side, and the other approached the driver's side. Both held flashlights, and rested their free hands on their revolvers holstered at their sides. "What are you doing here?"

"Pizza delivery, sir."

The officer shined his light on the door of the car. "Sal's Pizza. Coney Island's Best" had been hand painted in green and red. "Coney Island to Howard Beach. A bit far to be delivering a pizza. Where's it going?"

Moses got out of the car. "I have the address somewhere." He touched his pockets keeping his hands in plain sight. "I'm sorry, officer. I can't seem to find it."

The officer flashed his light across the back seat. "And I can't find the pizza. You guys are coming with me."

Rothman looked at the pristine yellow walls splattered with soapy water. He circled the tub. He squatted and looked up at it, then stood on a chair and looked down, examining the body from all angles. "Maybe we'll get lucky and it will turn out to have been an accident. Maybe she reached for the top of the low refrigerator to pull herself up, and grabbed the cord for the hotplate instead."

"I don't think so. She looks like she was in good shape. She didn't need anything to help her up. Besides," Cardello ran her hand over one of the ruffled pillows on the neatly made bed, "anyone who keeps a place as tidy and as organized as she did would be more careful than to have a wire dangling. The girl even put away her clothes before she stepped into the tub."

Cardello walked slowly around the apartment as she slipped on her gloves. Tucked neatly between the wall and a white dresser, was a row of four hooks. A mop and a dustpan occupied the first two. A broom hung from the next, and a purse hung on the last. "It wasn't robbery," she said, looking through the bag. "Wallet's still here. Three hundred bucks in it."

"The girl has a tortured expression on her face. Gruesome way to go. Did you ever see someone get fried?"

"Only in the movies."

"Several sets of prints out here," the officer dusting the outside sill reported. "I'll get them down to the lab, stat. Found this ball in the corner of the fire escape, too."

Rothman reached for the basketball the officer held out. He twirled it on his index finger. "She knew her assailant."

The paramedics left, and a dark blue van—with the words Kings County Hospital Mortuary Wagon stenciled in small letters on the side—pulled in near the hydrant. Residents had seen that van enough times at the projects to know what it said. A few minutes later, a station wagon pulled up. Flashing red lights illuminated the words, Crime Scene Investigation Unit, stenciled in large letters on the side door of the wagon. Then a car from the coroner's office pulled up. Two other men wheeled a gurney into the building, an empty body bag on it.

Everyone waited. The other tenants broke off into small groups on the sidewalk. "What happened?" "I heard…" "No, it was like this…" At first they whispered. But as their stories became more and more elaborate, their voices grew. Then the front door opened, and the men wheeled the gurney out. This time, the bag was full.

Chapter 23

The dining room table was set with the Rosenthal china on an immaculate white linen cloth. A side salad, a baked potato, broccoli, and the rib roast Mrs. Rollins had prepared earlier that day, exactly the way Mr. B liked it, sat cooling on the table.

Mrs. Rollins stood, arms crossed over her chest, heel tapping on the floor and eyes glued to the grandfather clock, when Brad Dawson came downstairs for dinner. "You know I serve promptly at seven. Now just look at this. The salad's wilted. The potato's ice cold, and the juices from the prime rib have congealed on the plate. I've spoken to you about this before, but you refuse to listen. My entire schedule is upset."

Brad took a deep breath. "Let's not go through all of this again, Mrs. Rollins."

"It wasn't enough that he was out of the picture. It was the girl you should have been pushing away, not me."

"My God, Mrs. Rollins. What are you saying? Her? Who?" Brad grabbed the housekeeper's arms and held her away from him. "You're ranting, woman. Make sense."

"You didn't come to me. You went to her. It was the morning after Keith's accident. I could tell by the expression on your face. You already knew."

Mallory had just walked down the stairs. She'd been about to enter the dining room when she caught the raised words, "Keith" and "accident" and "you already knew." Then she heard Mrs. Rollins say, "It was all your fault." She backed up against the wall near the doorway, and sucked in her breath. *What had the housekeeper meant? How could Brad have known? Unless…*

"Mrs. Rollins, that's enough."

But the old woman persisted. "I've been more than a housekeeper…"

"No. You *are* a housekeeper. I pay you to run my house, not to run my life."

Mallory was stunned. How could Brad have raised his voice to Mrs. Rollins?

The chastised woman hurried out of the dining room, through the hall, and up the stairs.

Chapter 24

Frank bit his last fingernail down to a stub. He picked at his cuticles until they bled. His nerves were raw. He'd had the baby since Tuesday. He'd wanted to bring her to his sister that same day he took her, but Charlotte wouldn't be home until Friday. He couldn't call and tell her about the baby, the replacement. Someone might hear.

He just had to keep her until Charlotte got back. He had planned to stop for diapers, and whatever else he needed, once he left Brooklyn, but now those plans were screwed up. He panicked when he realized he had just taken the last bottle from the refrigerator. He picked up the baby and fed her. "What do I do with you? I have to get more formula. Do I take you to the store, or leave you here alone?" Wizened eyes looked up at him. A little mouth curled into a tiny smile. Slowly, the baby closed her eyes. Frank made his decision. He would leave her here. That would be safer.

He put the sleeping infant back into the makeshift crib he'd put together, grabbed some money from his wallet, and ran to Rite Aid.

In his haste to get back to the unattended baby, he grabbed the measure-and-mix formula, rather than the ready-made kind. The baby began to stir as he returned to his apartment. He paced the floor carrying her. Back and forth, back and forth he walked until she dozed again.

"Just tonight. One more night. I can get through this," he said to himself. His hands shook as he spooned the powdered formula into a measuring cup. Outside, a truck backfired. He dropped the cup.

"Breathe, Frankie, breathe," he told himself. He tucked his trembling hands into his armpits. Still, he couldn't stop their involuntary shaking. He clenched his fists. "Breathe. The kid will be gone tomorrow. Your sister will be happy. No one else will know. Everything will be better tomorrow."

The phone rang. He grabbed it and answered fast.

"Meet me now, near Seaside Park," the gravelly voice said.

"No. You said no more. You said I'd repaid you. That I was finished. That Charlotte was safe."

The voice rattled off the location of the meeting place.

"But I'm on Murdock Street."

"Fifteen minutes. Don't make me wait."

Frank's hands raked through his hair. What could he do? He couldn't let anything happen to his sister. He peered down at the sleeping baby. "I'll be back soon. I have to go."

Car keys in hand, Frank ran down the stairs, two, then three at a time. He ran across the lawn, jumped the low hedge, and had his car in gear and moving before he could pull his left leg in and slam the door.

Thursday was summer concert night at Coney Island's Seaside Park. The crowds were beginning to leave now, to avoid the rush that would follow the show's coming finale. They surged onto Brighton Beach Avenue, bringing traffic to a standstill. And Frank, stuck in the middle, clenched his steering wheel. His knuckles turned white. Sweat poured from his forehead. The dashboard clock showed four minutes to go, then three. In a split second, he turned the wheel hard, accelerated, and jumped the curb.

Leaving his car on the pedestrian walk, he shoved his way through the throng, knocking lawn chairs and blankets out of arms until he finally reached the spot under the elevated train, a distance from the concert goers. He leaned forward. Lowering his head and resting his hands on his knees, he gasped for air.

A few minutes later, the sound of footsteps made Frank straighten up. He began to turn just as a figure emerged from the shadows.

"Don't turn around," the voice said.

Huge speakers amplified the show music for several blocks, and Frank cupped his left hand over his good ear to better hear.

"I promised to return the key case, the one with your fingerprints on it, and I always keep my promises." The figure threw the case at Frank. It landed at his feet.

"Now pick it up and put it in your pocket."

Frank did as he was told.

"Anyone see you pick up the girl?"

"No, there was just some blind guy at a window."

"How do you know he was blind?"

"I heard him saying, 'Ms. McGill is that you? Are you all right?'"

"So no one else knew about the baby… just you and the doctor."

"…and the guy on the phone. The doctor called someone about buying it. I listened from the window."

"Did you hear a name?"

"Dantano."

"You've done well, Frankie. I won't be needing your services any more."

Frank exhaled. And just as the Q train pulled into the station, and the music crescendoed, and thunderous applause erupted, a bullet ripped through his head.

Chapter 25

It had been years since Willard Thompson had any reason to celebrate... until today. His airline ticket, along with his money, banded together in several different envelopes, was secure in the hiding place beneath the floor boards. His luggage, under his cot, was packed and ready to go. His step light, he walked to the corner grocery, picked up a quart of Häagen-Dazs Chocolate Chocolate Chip ice cream, and headed home. His flight the following day would bring him to his new life in Anchorage, Alaska.

Out of habit, he looked around before turning into the alley. He opened the locks on the side door and entered. Quickly he turned the deadbolt from the inside. Then he laughed. He was done with all of this cloak-and-dagger stuff. He set the ice cream on the counter and pulled a spoon out of the drawer near the sink.

Vickie had introduced him to this ice cream. She'd bought a quart for them to share after he'd helped her out with her abortion. She knew about his plans for Alaska, but both had agreed that she didn't fit into them. She was determined to finish her education. His hand hesitated over the phone. Then he picked it up and dialed her number. A woman answered on the first ring.

"Hi, Vickie—"

"Who's calling, please," a female voice asked.

Thompson recognized Cardello's voice, and put down the phone. The ice cream, untouched, melted in its container on the counter.

Moses was right. Driving without a license got Dirk a night in juvie. But there was nothing they could hold Moses for, and after detaining him for a couple of hours, they let him go. It was near midnight, but he wasn't ready to call it a night.

He couldn't do anything for Dirk. And he had no wheels to get him back to Howard Beach to check around for the baby but, intent on finding out more about the abortionist Vickie's killer had mentioned, Moses headed back to Elgart Street. He turned into the alley next to where Eduardo had lived. He heard a lock being opened, then another and another. Thompson emerged from his apartment. A dim light silhouetted him and a bundle he carried. Moses flattened himself on the ground. His dark clothing and skin made him invisible as he huddled beside the building, listening for Thompson to lock the door. But he didn't.

The man looked both ways and then, package in hand, climbed through the broken chain-link fence that separated the alley from the trash-filled lot next door. Moses watched from the other side of the fence. Most of the lot was bathed in moonlight, and he had no trouble seeing Thompson put the package down and pull a small gardening shovel from his pocket before he began to dig through the debris.

The ground was hard, and the digging slow.

Moses calculated that he had only a few minutes before Thompson finished what he was doing and returned.

Noiselessly, he climbed the three steps and let himself into the side door of the dimly lit apartment. A low whistle escaped from his lips.

In an instant, he took in the surgical table, the stainless steel utility cart with its assortment of medical equipment nearby, and the empty intravenous bag dangling from a drip stand. To his left, against the wall, was a cot, and to his right, under the window, a sink with the kind of faucets doctors turn on with their elbows, to keep sterile. "You might fool the cops with your lying shit, but you're a mechanic like I'm a magician," he said, lifting one of the stirrups at the foot of the examination table.

Opposite Moses, one small, narrow room held a pull-chain toilet. The other room, next to it, appeared to be a pantry. On the wall to his left were two other doors. Quickly, he opened the first.

In what appeared to have been a living room, an old sofa was wedged against another door toward the front of the building. And dusty cloths covered musty-smelling pieces of furniture. Judging by the stained mattress that leaned against the wall, the other, slightly smaller room, with its door ajar, appeared to have been a bedroom. The rest of the room was bare, except for something in the center covered with a clean white sheet. Moses flipped on his pen light and peered under the cloth. His light reflected off the stainless steel of an incubator. Surprised by his find, Moses forgot his cardinal rule—stay alert.

*   *   *

Thompson finished digging the shallow hole. He unwrapped the package and lovingly touched his old medical bag. Then he re-wrapped it and placed it in the hole. "My old life is gone. Dead. It can be no more," he pronounced sadly, burying the bag. He piled broken cinder blocks on the mound, and topped it off with garbage that he scraped up with a piece of lumber.

Moses barely had time to hide behind the partially open door when Thompson entered the apartment. The man went directly to the sink, and turned on the water. Moses watched as he scrubbed his hands, and then his arms clear up to his elbows, just like the surgeons on TV did. Then he walked out of Moses' view. Moses moved the door a tiny bit to see. A garment bag on a hook behind it swayed, and he grabbed it to keep it still as he watched Thompson slip out of his clothes, pick up a book, and lay down on a cot against the wall.

Moses realized there was no way he could get out while the guy was there. He was trapped. Pushing aside cobwebs, he crawled under the leaning mattress. He'd bide his time, wait for the man to fall asleep.

While Moses lay hidden under the mattress in Thompson's apartment, Mallory tossed and turned on hers. She couldn't sleep. She got out of bed, intending to go to the kitchen to make a cup of tea. The door to Mrs. Rollins' sewing room was ajar. Something was burning. Mallory peered through the opening. Mrs. Rollins was sitting at the grandfather's ornate, drop-front desk. She crumpled a fistful of papers and released them from her hand. They fell into a small metal wastebasket, where flames reached up to consume them. Then she crumpled more paper.

Mallory opened the door. "I'm sorry, Mrs. Rollins, but I smelled smoke…"

"I was just burning a few papers. No need to concern yourself." Mrs. Rollins ran her fingers over the carved decorative trim of the desk.

"You must have loved the grandfather," Mallory said. "Wanting his desk and all." She walked over to touch it herself.

In answer, Mrs. Rollins' lips curled, but not into what Mallory would call a smile.

Then, almost immediately, that strange look left her face, and she turned her attention to Mallory. "Are you all right, child?"

Mallory leaned against the doorpost and sighed. "I just feel so… so helpless. And this…" She touched her engorged breasts, her shirt damp from the milk that leaked, "hurts so much… But you wouldn't understand."

"Why not? I was married once. I was a mother."

Surprise spread across Mallory's face. Even though she called the housekeeper Mrs. Rollins, she'd never pictured her as a wife or a mother. She'd assumed that the old woman had always worked for the grandfather, and then for Brad.

"I was too young to be married—to be a mother. My husband worked long hours. Stuck with a kid. Just four walls to look at. I swear I would have gone crazy if I stayed home one more day. I hired a sitter and got involved with a theater group in Brooklyn Heights. I had always wanted to be on stage, but they made me do makeup, help with costumes." A reflective look came over her, and for an instant her face softened. "That's where I met the Professor…"

"The professor?"

Mrs. Rollins pulled down the same basket that Mallory had recently tipped over. She shuffled through the papers, and pulled out a head shot from amongst the playbills in the basket. She held it up for Mallory to see. "The Professor. I worshiped this man, devoured every word out of his mouth. Pearls of wisdom he tossed my way." She gazed at the photograph, and her expression turned to one of scorn. "The bastard. A has-been. A stinking old actor.

"In the beginning, he fooled me with his stories of grandeur, of playing before royalty all over the world." She ripped the photo in half. Then ripped the two halves in half again. A restrained laugh escaped her lips. "I once thought he was a god. I had him up on a pedestal so high it strained my neck to look up at him." She ripped the pieces yet again, and watched them flutter into the wastebasket.

"One evening, he asked me to go with him and I did."

"Go with him?" Mallory, lost in her own thoughts, had lost the flow of Mrs. Rollins' story.

"He was going on the road with a touring company."

"And you left your family, just like that?"

"I didn't even go home to pack my clothes." She shrugged. "I was young. But at the time…" she took the playbills from the basket, and tossed them, one at a time, onto the desk. "Boston, Cincinnati, Seattle. We traveled across the country and back again."

She collected the playbills, and threw them carelessly back into the container.

"I was so naive. I thought that, if I just saw to his clothes and such, and waited, he'd come back to me." She laughed a contemptuous laugh. "He came back, all right. Most nights he came back drunk and just passed out, but occasionally, he'd remember I was there, and make love to me.

"By the time I realized the mistake I'd made in leaving my husband and child, it was too late. He had divorced me and found someone else.

"Things went from bad to worse. I got pregnant. And then the Professor threw me out of the house—in my eighth month."

Mallory bent over, holding her breasts firmly to her. "I'm sorry, but they hurt so much. The doctor offered to give me something—to dry up my milk, but I refused. I need to pump it—to save it for my baby." She breathed deeply. "I will find her, you know."

Rollins stood up, and turned her back to Mallory. "No one ever told me how to alleviate the pain of my engorged breasts," she said under her breath.

"Mrs. Rollins, I just don't understand. Why won't Brad help me? Why won't he believe me?"

Rollins spun back to face Mallory. "Child, Mr. B's brother is gone. Even though they had their differences, this was his brother's baby—would have been his niece—she's gone, too. And you can't, or won't, tell him what happened to the baby. Can you blame him for acting that way?"

"*My* baby is gone, too. *My* baby," Mallory screamed. "And I didn't do anything. I'm certain I didn't." Dizzy, she grabbed hold of the desk. "You've got to believe me."

The housekeeper walked to the window. She straightened a crease in the perfect drape, then moved it aside, and peered out the window.

"You do believe me, don't you?"

The old woman didn't answer.

"Mrs. Rollins?"

"It doesn't matter what I believe."

"Yes it does. You practically raised Keith, and Brad. You knew how excited Keith was about this baby. You knew how excited we both were. Why would I…"

"You're young. You'll get over this. You'll have other babies."

"How can you say that so… so… flippantly?"

Mrs. Rollins sighed. "There's nothing here for you, any more. Don't you see that?"

"You're telling me to run away?"

"No, child. Not run away. Just leave… Look, you're not well. The police will keep questioning you, over and over again. You won't be strong enough. For Keith's memory, let me help you get a new start. I've saved some money…"

"I'm not running away. I'll tell you again. I heard my baby crying. She's alive, and I'm going to find her. Things are coming back to me. I will remember. I will."

Mrs. Rollins let the drape fall back into place.

Chapter 26

The flushing of the toilet woke Moses. But he lay like a dead possum, barely breathing until he heard the man washing and brushing his teeth. Only when he was sure that the running water would muffle his sounds did he crawl out from under the mattress. He inched toward the door, from where he had observed the man earlier. The apartment was dark except for the dim lamp on the small table beside the cot. He had no idea of the time.

Thompson's phone rang. The incoming call made him halt. Then, hesitatingly, he walked toward the small table. Caller ID told him the call was from the lawyer. He pulled at his beard. His hand reached for the phone, then pulled away. "I'm out of here tomorrow," he said, backing away from it. "I'm not picking up this call." He let it ring until voice mail took over.

"Mr. Dawson isn't very happy with the outcome of your last assignment. If you know what's good for you, you'll pick up your phone now," the lawyer's assistant said.

Thompson stared at the phone. He chewed on his thumbnail. "Don't make me come to you," the voice said. Thompson's heart began to race.

He lowered himself to the cot and lifted the phone. "I, uh, was just getting up. What seems to be the problem?"

"Mr. Dawson doesn't like what he's hearing, *Doctor* Thompson."

"What are you talking about," Thompson asked.

"He paid you to do an abortion."

"And I did. Just like you told me to."

"Oh really?" The voice rose. "We know about your double dipping."

"I don't know what you're talking about."

"I think you do. Is it Radcliffe your daughter is attending?"

"You wouldn't…"

Thanks to the Internet, Thompson had found his daughter. While he'd never contacted her, using the name of a Radcliffe alumnus, he'd friended her and begun following her on Facebook.

"Please. She doesn't even know I'm alive. She has nothing to do with any of this."

"Funny the lengths some people will go to for their children, isn't it?"

"No. You're wrong. I wouldn't…"

"Thompson, you fuck with Dawson and… the girl said she heard the kid crying. It was alive."

"She was so drugged up she didn't even know where she was. Besides, I took care of it."

"You're lying."

Sweat broke out on Thompson's forehead. Pain cursed through his chest. He fumbled for the aspirin bottle that was always in his pocket. Trembling, he popped two into his mouth.

"Does the name Dantano ring a bell?"

The bottle fell. The other pills scattered over the floor. He clutched his chest, panting small, rapid breaths.

"I asked you a question," the voice on the phone grew louder.

"Jesus Christ. All right. I'll tell you." Thompson paused to catch his breath. "Do you know what a late-term abortion entails?"

"I don't need to know."

"An implement is inserted into the woman's vagina while the fetus is still in her womb. It punctures the skull. Next—"

"Shut up, Thompson. Shut up."

"—the brains are sucked out. A dead fetus is easier to remove from the woman's—"

"Shut up."

"No. I won't shut up." Thompson breathed deeply. "Enough is enough. We had an arrangement, and I did my part. I'm finished now."

"I have more money for you."

"I said I'm through." Thompson hit the red button, ending the call. He ripped the cord from the wall, and threw the phone across the room.

The man's gravelly voice on the other end was so loud that Moses heard the whole conversation. His eyes opened wide. "So Dawson's involved with Dantano, the baby buyer." I have to warn Ms. McG," he said to himself.

From the slit near the doorjamb, Moses watched as Thompson pulled a folding knife from his pocket, and advanced toward the partially open door—and toward Moses. Moses froze in place. How could the man know he was there? Moses' heart beat louder as each footstep grew nearer. Then, just outside the room, Thompson stopped and kneeled down. Moses let out his breath. Thompson pried up two floorboards, and pulled out a bunch of envelopes, banded together.

He took them to the table, then he pulled a piece of luggage out from under the cot. "Alaska, here I come," he said, kissing the airline ticket he removed from one of the envelopes. Leaving one money-stuffed envelope and the airline ticket aside, he put the rest into his luggage. Then he turned back toward Moses. Moses raised a knee, prepared to kick the door open and flee if the man entered the room, but he didn't. Instead, Thompson stopped at the doorway. He reached around, grabbed the garment bag, and returned to the table. He pulled a suit and shirt from the bag and dressed. Then, turning his back to Moses, he slid the envelope and his cell phone into his jacket pockets.

Moses saw his chance. He opened the bedroom door and bolted across the kitchen toward the side door.

Thompson turned, startled to see tall, black boy. He grabbed the drip stand beside him and, holding his luggage in one hand, awkwardly balanced the stand in the other. "Who are you? How did you get in here? What do you want?"

"Easy, man. Easy," Moses said, putting his empty hands out in front of him. "I don't mean you no harm. I thought this place was deserted. Jus' came in here to get some sleep. I don't know nothin'. Honest."

Thompson took a step back and raised the stand. But before he could fling it, the younger, more agile Moses, had twisted it from his hand and flung it across the room.

Moses seized a scalpel from the utility cart just as the stand hit the wall with a loud clatter. He pinned Thompson against the surgical table, holding the scalpel to his neck. "Where's the baby?"

Thompson raised his hand protectively. "Please," he said.

Moses brought the scalpel closer. "Where?"

"I don't know."

The blade nicked his neck.

"I had it," the frightened man blurted out. "Then someone took it. Honest. But look, I'll give you this." Without taking his eyes off Moses, or letting go of the luggage still in his left hand, Thompson slowly lowered his right hand and reached into the inside pocket of his jacket. He pulled out an envelope and, raising it to his mouth, ripped it open with his teeth. "See. It's yours. All of it," he said, spilling the contents at Moses' feet.

Moses glanced down, surprised at the number of bills lying on the ground. In that instant, Thompson brought his arm up, and the scalpel flew from Moses' hand. At the same time, he swung his bag at Moses. Moses fell. His head hit the base of the surgical table.

Thompson turned to leave, then looked back at the boy, lying still on the floor. He put his luggage down, got to his knees, and put his fingers on the boy's neck. Only after he found a pulse did he carefully roll the boy toward him. He tilted Moses' head back, and put his ear to the boy's nose. The airway was clear. Relieved, Thompson pulled a blanket from the cot and covered Moses.

He gathered the money he'd spilled to the floor, and picked up his bag.

Just as he was about to let himself out, Moses moaned. Thompson turned back to him. "No. It's too soon. You can't get up yet. I can't let you ruin this for me. I've waited too long to be free again." He took a role of surgical tape out of the drawer in the utility cart. "Please understand," he said. Bending down, he grabbed the boy's arms and taped them behind his back. Next he taped Moses' ankles, and then put tape over his mouth. "Don't worry, I'll let the authorities know where you are just before my plane takes off."

Chapter 27

The smell of the paper Mrs. Rollins was burning paper made Mallory ill. Forgetting about the tea she'd gotten up to make, she went back to her room and collapsed on the bed. The soft feather pillows and cool, crisp comforter enveloped her body, but she couldn't sleep. Her mind spun, faster and faster. Kaleidoscope pictures, words, places, people. A jumble —blending, changing noises—loud, soft, blurred.

Mrs. Rollins' voice and the crunching of paper—paper crinkling, louder and louder—echoed in her head.

Something had to come back to her. Maybe if she retraced her steps again.

Mallory cut through the hedges to where she had left Keith's car earlier that day. She retraced the streets she had driven with Moses. Back and forth she drove. On Elgart Street, two street lights were out, and she slowed down. Her headlights caught the reflector of a bike pedal. She jammed on her break just in time to avoid a bicyclist. One of the overhead streetlights blinked off, and then on again.

A flash of light, then darkness. The feeling of a coarse cover slipping over her face. Yes. That happened just before she was dragged into a dark, narrow place. She sat, frozen in her seat, until a car whizzing past with blaring stereo brought her back to the present.

Trembling, cold and sweating, she pulled over to the curb. Her heart pounding, her breath shallow, she studied the row of houses. There was only one house with an alley: the first one. All of the others were attached on both sides. She stepped out of the car, and walked around to the curb. The windows on the porch were boarded up. The house was dark, the alley darker still. But not even her childhood terror of dark places could keep her from finding her baby.

She took one small step after another. Into the black musty passage. Remembering the familiar odor, her courage rose. "I can do this. I can. I can," she said, over and over. "I have to know." She reached out in the darkness. Her hand touched the rough concrete wall. "I scraped the back of my hand on the wall, this wall."

Using the wall to guide her, she inched her way slowly down the alley. The light flashed on, and then off again. The alley went from black to dim. Almost at the end of the alley, she felt a step. And then two others. Another flashback came to her. Her back hitting each of those three steps as she'd been half dragged, half carried up into the house. This house. That would account for the bruises on her backside.

She made her way up the stairs in the dark. Her hand found the door knob. She banged on the door. Then she kicked it and shook the handle. Nothing. She slid her hand up the door. Three deadbolt locks. The door was locked. It was no use. No one was there.

Muffled sounds, as though he was under water, came to Moses through the locked door. His arms and legs, tightly bound, prevented him from sitting up. He tried to raise his head. Dizzy, he sunk back to the floor. The tape over his mouth pulled and prevented him from calling anything other than "mmmm, mmmm." He had to attract the attention of whoever was outside. In the dim lamplight, he made out the drip stand leaning against the wall, and although restrained, he wiggled to it, and knocked it over. It clattered to the floor. Then he lay silent, listening for a response to his noise.

Mallory tripped and fell as she turned to leave. In what seemed to her like slow motion, she rolled down the steps. She lay still for an instant. Had she heard something? Noise coming from the apartment? *Probably just a ringing in my ears, or my own scream as I fell,* she thought. Defeated, she dragged herself back to the car, and went back to Brad's house.

Chapter 28

The house was dark when Mallory returned later that night. She pulled her aching body up the stairs. She crawled into bed, but lay awake recounting every moment, every detail of the last three days. She began with Monday night, when the car picked her up. But she had no memory of the car ride—after the driver passed the hospital. No. She had to jump to Tuesday.

On Tuesday, she'd woken in the hospital, her breasts full, her belly empty. Detectives asking her what she'd done with her baby.

On Wednesday, Brad had brought her to his house. He told her not to leave, but she'd sneaked back to her apartment. He'd come after her, taken her keys, brought her back to his house again, and she was locked in the bedroom.

Then today, the detectives had spent a long time questioning her. Said they'd found her car at the creek. How could that be? She had to make them believe her so they'd look for the person who was really responsible for Eloise's disappearance. But how? Her only clue was the background sounds she'd heard on the news. But she couldn't be certain if they were reminiscent of the ones she heard that night, and she couldn't just tell the detectives she heard noises. They already thought she was crazy. At least, Detective Cardello did.

But memories were coming back. Being grabbed and pulled from a car. A light going on and off. The boarded-up house. She'd been certain that was where she'd been taken. But it turned out to be a dead end. Only new bruises to show for her search.

Friday, July 16
Chapter 29

Dawn was just beginning to break when Mallory walked into the kitchen. She flipped on the light, surprised to find Brad sitting in the dark room. He glanced at her, then turned away. He left the table, went to the stove, and poured a fresh cup of coffee. Her greeting died on her lips. How different things were now.

Soon after Keith had died, over a cup of coffee, on an early morning just like this, Brad had told her about his lonely childhood. He'd told her about his adoring father and the cold, uncaring mother who had abandoned him. He told her about his new stepmother, and how she'd presented him with Keith, his baby brother. And he told her about his devastation when his parents died in a car accident, leaving him and Keith orphaned.

She took a deep breath. "Brad, can we talk? Please."

Brad turned from the stove. "What is there to talk about? Mallory, if you didn't want the baby, why didn't you give her to me? She was my brother's. I would have brought her up. Loved her. At least then, I'd have had a part of my brother." Brad headed out of the kitchen, coffee cup in hand.

Mallory ran after him, and grabbed his arm. "Brad, please."

He wrenched his arm away. Hot coffee splattered across the sleeve of his blue oxford shirt. "What do you want from me?"

"I want you to help me find my baby. You said you would."

"That was when I thought you were telling me the truth."

"I've never lied to you."

Brad went to the sink, and spilled out the remainder of his coffee, before turning to face Mallory. "Did you just happen to forget that you and my brother were married?"

"My God, Brad, I'll never forget. I wanted to tell you. Keith and I were going to tell you right after we told you about the baby, but your grandfather started planning a large wedding. He was so excited."

"And after Keith died?"

Mallory sat down. "What was the use, then? He was gone. All I could think about was my baby, Keith's baby."

"And since she was going to be a Dawson, her inheritance?"

"That's crazy Brad."

"Is it? You were looking for the will. My grandfather's will."

"No."

"Then tell me why you were going through my office drawers."

"I wasn't. I only opened the box on top of your desk to find the keys to Keith's car."

"So why was this in my drawer?" Dawson pulled Mallory's plastic charm bracelet from his pocket.

Mallory grabbed her left wrist. It was bare. "I don't know."

"I do. Mrs. Rollins found it there when she was filing some papers for me. I should have listened to her when she told me you were a scheming—"

"Brad, you can't possibly believe that. Just listen to yourself. You're not making any sense. If I was thinking in terms of an inheritance, wouldn't I have told you about our marriage immediately? And why would I do away with my own baby, who would be the heir? But you, on the other hand… Oh, my God." Mallory's eyes filled with fear. They opened wide. She stood up. Slowly, she backed away from him.

"I heard you say, 'Everything went exactly as planned. She has no clue. I'll take care of the loose ends.' What did you mean?"

"That wasn't about you," Brad's surprise was evident. "It was one of my big clients. Her husband asked me to secure a yacht for him, to arrange a surprise party for his wife."

"Well… Why did you say I couldn't go back to my apartment?"

"Mallory, think clearly. Did I ever say that?"

"Not to me directly. But Mrs. Rollins told me you did."

"And what else did she say?"

"That you said I couldn't leave the area."

"Wasn't it the detectives who said you couldn't leave the area? When you were in the hospital?"

Mallory rubbed her brow, trying hard to remember. "Why did you want me sedated, locked in the room?"

"What are you saying?"

"The pills Mrs. Rollins gave me. You told her to."

"I don't know what you're talking about."

Mallory didn't respond. Instead, she ran out the back door.

Chapter 30

A closing car door broke the morning stillness. Cardello came awake instantly. "You're getting too old to be spending the night in the car. You should know better," she chastised herself as she stretched. "This was a dumb idea." Then she looked at the glowing hands on her watch, 5:30 A.M. She was about to reach for her thermos to fortify herself with some black coffee, as Mallory ran down the path and up the block.

Cardello started her engine, and, without turning on her headlights, followed the girl to the dark Toyota parked around the corner.

Mallory drove toward Coney Island. She turned on the street near Nathan's, and parked adjacent to the beach. She walked up the ramp to the boardwalk and headed for the pier that stuck out into the water, near the stadium.

Cardello followed at a safe distance. After Mallory sat down, the detective jogged down the boardwalk and onto the pier. "Hi," she said, as though she'd run into Mallory by accident while on an early morning run. "Mind if I join you?"

"Suit yourself."

Cardello lowered herself to the bench. Mallory turned away from the detective, toward the golden sun materializing over the horizon, the sea gulls standing, statues on the bronzed sand, the men fishing at the tip of the pier, a distance away. But none of it registered.

She breathed in the salty air, then turned back to Cardello. "Look, I know you don't believe me. I can't explain my car being at the creek. I can't explain why I was there. But I know I didn't hurt my baby."

"Losing the man you love: a shock like that could make a woman do just about anything."

"You're wrong, Detective Cardello," Mallory said, jumping up. "Keith was my breath, my heartbeat, my best friend—and my baby was a part of him. You can't know how badly I wanted her."

"I only meant—"

"Don't play your mind games with me. You couldn't understand."

Mallory touched the back of the bench. "I used to come here with Keith. This was our bench." Her voice caught. "We sat here planning our lives together: where we would live, how many children we would have…. Now it's up to me. I know our daughter is out there somewhere, and I'm going to find her." She turned toward the sea, and rested her elbows on the railing.

Several terns flew over, drawing her attention to them.

"I stayed at Brad's those first few weeks after Keith died. I went through my waking hours in a daze. But the nights were the worst. I kept seeing Keith. It was as though he was trying to tell me something, only I couldn't understand what.

"When I returned to my old apartment, I locked myself in, and sat in the rocker I'd bought at a flea market. Not rocking. Just sitting, hugging the carnival bear Keith had won for me." Mallory raised her arms to her tender breasts. "Brad tells me I wouldn't answer the telephone or the door bell. I went without food, drink, sleep. I didn't bathe. I had no idea how many days passed that way. Then I felt that first small flutter. A tiny foot, maybe, or an elbow nudging me. And I remembered the child I carried." Mallory's arms caressed her vacant stomach. "It was her first flutter that brought me back to life after Keith died. Every waking moment revolved around that life growing in me. I felt myself gaining strength I'd never known I possessed. I got up, showered, and made myself some tea and toast. Then I crawled into my bed and slept. Twelve hours later, I woke with the courage to get on with my life, and to prepare for the new life I was carrying. I cleaned my apartment, set up my easel, and pulled out the unfinished portrait I'd been commissioned to do before Keith's death.

"I'd been an orphan since I was seven. My mother and I were walking when the car jumped the curb. She pushed me out of the way, but the car… there wasn't enough time for her. I survived." She ran her fingers over the faint scar on her cheek. "Seven-year-olds are resilient. My mother protected me, but I let something happen to my baby, my Eloise—and I don't even know what.

"I endured the foster care system for eleven years. Until I was eighteen, I was a ward of the state and then, over the next nine years, I worked at any menial job I could find to put myself through school. And all that time, I dreamed of finding a wonderful man and having a family of my own. Don't you see, knowing that I carried Keith's baby was the only thing that sustained me during those first months alone."

Cardello got up, and turned Mallory to face her. She looked closely into Mallory's eyes.

"You were right. Your case sounded so… so cut and dried. I didn't believe you. But hearing you speak of Keith… I do understand that kind of love. Mallory, just give me something. Anything. Make me believe you. Tell me whatever you can."

"My God, this is all such a nightmare. First Keith, and then my baby. Disjointed pieces are coming back to me. The sounds that night—I remember someone dragging me. That's why I was driving around Coney Island yesterday, when the police picked me up. There were screams from the roller coaster, and cheering from the ball park. I was there. That driver took me there. It was like a nightmare, but I think it was true."

People were cheering. Pain was ripping through my body, and people were cheering. You've got to believe me."

"Are you telling me that someone wanted to take your baby," Cardello asked slowly.

Mallory shrugged. She thought of Brad, of the things she'd accused him of, and of the accusations he'd thrown at her, but they were so unbelievable, and too painful for her to share.

Chapter 31

Rothman's night at home had been no more restful than Cardello's in the car. Images of Mallory McGill ran through his mind. He just knew she was innocent. He'd developed a sixth sense over the years, but what was he missing? There had to be something. A piece to the puzzle. He dressed and, needing caffeine, drove past Rachel's store. She wasn't open. What had he expected? It was only six. He was at his desk at the station moments later. Tossing the files for the overdosed kid and the electrocuted woman aside, he opened the McGill file. He rolled the large chalkboard out from the corner, and studied his notes for what must have been the hundredth time.

The clock read 6:10 A.M. as Cardello dragged herself into the office.

"You look like hell," Rothman said.

"Don't get all bitchy on me, Sam. That car was damned uncomfortable all night. And I'm telling you now, if I don't get home this evening, Nadine will kill me, and you'll have another homicide on your hands."

Rothman got up and poured Cardello a large cup of black coffee. "Peace?"

She looked up as he handed it to her. "Sam, you look like shit yourself."

"I'm just so damned frustrated. You'd think we'd get lucky with one of these," Rothman grabbed the file from his desk. "This McGill case is haunting me. I know you think she's guilty, but what if you're wrong? What if her baby is still alive? This is day number four. Time has to be running out."

Cardello lowered her tired frame into her chair, and sipped her coffee. "I'm not so certain any more. You may be right about her innocence. You know I didn't believe her, but when I talked to her this morning, over on the pier, I got a different feeling. When she talked about her boyfriend… Well, she was so… so sincere. I would have known if she was putting it on."

Sargent Lazaro flung open the door, knocking the file out of his hand.

"Why the hell don't you look where you're going?"

"No time for chit chat. Got another homicide for you. A body under the el. Ocean Parkway and Brighton Beach Avenue."

Rothman ran his fingers through his unkempt hair and yawned.

"We're both getting too old for all of this crap," Cardello said as she dragged herself out of her seat.

The crime scene unit was already in action mapping things out when Cardello and Rothman arrived. They flashed their badges, and a uniformed officer held up the yellow tape that cordoned off the area. They ducked their heads down, and walked under it.

"Hey, you guys, long time no see." Paulie came over to shake their hands.

Rothman looked at the van parked nearby with the Channel 12 logo on it. "This is just great. What do those guys have? A private line to homicide?"

"Don't laugh," Paulie said. "That's a big problem in the crime scene unit. Someone's been leaking out information."

"So what have you got for us, Paulie?"

"A gunshot wound to the head," Paulie's voice rose, but he couldn't compete with the deafening noise of the Q train roaring into the station overhead.

Rothman motioned him to wait.

"No sign of a weapon. Our guys are checking the sewers now," he finished, as the train pulled away from the station.

"Deploying more cops to the city's high-crime hot spots sure hasn't helped our crime rates any. How long's he been dead?" Cardello asked.

"Well, the muscles begin stiffening after around three hours—"

"Don't quote me from your Mortuary Science classes. Just give me an answer."

"Seven hours, maybe eight." He looked at his watch. "Probably happened around ten or eleven last night. Some woman was leaving her boyfriend's place when she saw the body."

Cardello studied the no parking signs.

"Parking restrictions for concert nights are relaxed. Cars park under the el, diagonally—some for the whole night." Paulie looked up and pointed. "And these street lights are broken. It's easy to see how the crowds could have missed a body slumped between those two cars in the dark."

Cardello nodded. "Any identification?"

"All we found on him was a single key, and a key case."

"What else can you tell us?"

"I think you might want to see this." Using a pencil, he lifted the long hair on the right side of the corpse's head. It was missing an ear.

Cardello winced.

Rothman pulled out his flashlight and squatted to get a closer look. "Bits of a dry adhesive around the opening," he said. "My guess is that if he had a prosthesis, he wasn't wearing it when he got here. But have your boys look around for that, too."

Several hours passed before Cardello and Rothman could get away from the precinct to grab a good cup of coffee. Rothman pulled up to the curb in front of the Rachel's.

Cardello's cell phone rang as they entered the shop.

"Detective Cardello, it's Mallory McGill. After we talked this morning, I remembered something else."

"Yes, I'm listening."

"It sounds bizarre. Even to me, but I was in the car and having a contraction. The driver passed the hospital. I screamed for him to stop, but he wouldn't listen. He kept driving. I leaned forward to grab his shoulder, to make him stop. And this is what I just remembered. When he turned to me, the car jerked. I grabbed his ear instead of his shoulder. And his ear came off in my hand...."

"His ear?" Cardello looked at Rothman. "Can you tell me which one?"

"It was the right ear. You do believe me, don't you?"

"What happened after that?"

"I can't remember. I keep trying, but I can't."

"We'll talk again later. Keep trying." Cardello put down her phone and turned to Rothman. "McGill said the driver's ear came off in her hand. This can't be a coincidence. How many corpses do we come across with missing ears?"

Rachel squeezed her ample frame behind the counter. She turned on the television, and started a fresh pot of coffee brewing.

"…more than the traditional Thursday night concerts have captivated the public's interest in Coney Island," the announcer was saying. "Murders seem to be on the rise in the neighborhood. The latest victim—"

Rachel returned with two cups of coffee. "That's something about last night's murder, isn't it? The guy they found on Brighton Beach Avenue, with his ear missing?"

"Rachel, they had that on the radio? About his ear missing? You knew about that already?"

"I heard it at nine. I have my morning coffee with the news—Channel 12. But they've been running the same story all day. The stiff with the missing ear bumped the McGill story from the top spot."

"Damn." Cardello slapped the counter. "I talk to McGill on the boardwalk and I get nothing. She goes home and suddenly she remembers an ear? How convenient. She *borrowed* this information. Can't you see? From the news. This is just another part of her fantasy. Double damn, I hate to be played for a fool."

"Wait, Teri. We don't know for sure. Maybe she didn't hear the broadcast. Maybe this was the guy who picked her up."

"And maybe the doctor just forgot that she came for her appointment." Cardello searched her pocket, and popped a piece of gum into her mouth. She spun the worn vinyl seat of the swivel stool around and around. "Or maybe she's a fuckin' good little actress."

"Let's stop at the hospital."

Chapter 32

Mallory, shaken by Detective Cardello's words, had remained sitting on the pier as the officer returned to her car. She'd said, "If what you say is true, then someone *wanted* to take your baby. Why?"

Everything led to Brad, but could she really believe that?

An hour later, stiff from sitting, Mallory returned to his house. She took a chocolate chip cookie from the jar that Mrs. Rollins kept filled, and sat down at the kitchen table. Vaguely aware of the cookie in her hand, she tried to put the pieces together.

Last night, Mrs. Rollins accused Brad of knowing about Keith's accident—before the news got out. How would he have known? Unless it was no accident. Could Brad have been jealous of Keith? He told me that he and Keith were close. But Mrs. Rollins told me they had their differences.

And how had Brad known that Keith and I had been married? Mallory jumped up from the chair. "Unless he went through my papers," she said aloud.

"Maybe I have to do the same thing: go through his papers to find out what he was hiding."

Brad's car was gone, and Mrs. Rollins had begun her cleaning upstairs. Mallory heard the vacuum cleaner running. She put the uneaten cookie down, and pushed her chair away from the table.

She tiptoed into Brad's office, and sat at his desk. She ran her hands over the mahogany top, cool to the touch, and bare except for a leather-bound writing tablet, a Mont Blanc pen, a telephone, and the lacquered box where Brad kept his keys. She hesitated, then, in turn, opened and closed each of the neatly organized drawers. She spun around on Brad's barrel-back leather chair until she faced the credenza behind the desk. A flat-screen monitor shared the cabinet top with several potted violets, a Rolodex card file, the *New York Times* and the *Wall Street Journal*.

Mallory ran her fingers over the 3x5 cards in the open file tray. All lined up except for one near the back. She pulled out the card labeled "F.

Assanato, Murdock Street." On the top right side of the card, in small letters, was written "OBT." A small black X crossed those letters. As she returned the card to its place, she noticed the next one. "V. Davis, Mermaid Avenue." This card also had the same OBT in the upper right corner, and an X also covered those letters. She flipped through the remaining cards in the tray, and found six others with the letters OBT on them. But none of those had been crossed out.

Lifting her head, she listened. Mrs. Rollins was still running the vacuum cleaner. She opened the file cabinet, pulled out the eight files that matched the cards, and carried them over to Brad's club chair in the corner of the room. She couldn't see the doorway from there, but the light was better, and she could still hear the hum of the vacuum. She breathed deeply of the new leather as she settled in to read the files.

F. Assanato was the first. The tab on his file was labeled "manslaughter." The others were marked things like "malpractice," "soliciting," and "tax evasion," and all said "pro bono." *If Brad provided legal services to people who were unable to afford them, might OBT have something to do with that,* Mallory wondered.

What caught Mallory's full attention, though, was the one for W. Thompson. The original street address had been whited out, and a new address penciled in. The address was faint, but Mallory caught the street name: Elgart. That was one of the streets she and Moses had driven down. And that was the street with the boarded-up house.

There was a sudden quiet in the house. The vacuum had been turned off. Quickly, she slipped the files under the cushion of the chair, and hurried into the kitchen.

When Mrs. Rollins came down, Mallory was sitting and waiting for the tea kettle to whistle.

"I'm making my grocery list," the housekeeper said, bringing a pad and pencil to the table. "Is there anything special you would like, child?"

Mallory shook her head. Food was the last thing on her mind.

Every Friday morning, Mrs. Rollins prepared her shopping list. Mallory sat quietly watching, anxious for her to be done and gone. Efficiently, the housekeeper began with meats and poultry, went on to fruits and vegetables, and ended with cleaning supplies and miscellaneous. Mallory had accompanied her on occasion and knew that she'd head down Nostrand Avenue to Pathmark for basics, then cross the street and go to Silver Star for her meats and poultry. After she brought the perishables home, and put them in the refrigerator, she'd take a shopping cart and walk to the green grocer on Avenue M for fruits and vegetables.

There was something comforting about her routine that never varied. And today, Mallory noticed something familiar about her writing. Especially the first letters of the words tomatoes, oranges, and bananas, TOB. Mallory mixed up the letters: BTO. Then mixed them again: OBT. That was it. The letters were familiar because they were the ones printed on Brad's pro bono files—in the same handwriting.

Well, why not? Mallory thought. *Mrs. Rollins helps Brad with his office work. If only I could ask her what those letters mean, but then I'd have to tell her that I'd been snooping.*

Chapter 33

Cardello sipped her coffee as Rothman drove to Coney Island Hospital. "I'm sorry, Sam. I know how you feel, but my little walk at the creek yesterday might just have given us the evidence we need to close the McGill case. I've asked the lab to put a rush on it."

Rothman pulled into the parking lot. "Let's see what information her doctor can give us." They entered the lobby and the detectives flashed their badges at security. The hospital tried to release as many patients as possible on Fridays, to lighten the weekend load. Still, a large group of restless visitors waited on the roped-off line for the slow moving elevators. Cardello cut in front, and she and Rothman got on the first one to come. On the eighth floor, signs in English, Spanish, Russian, and Arabic read OB/GYN Clinic 8N26. Near the Women's Health Center, machines dispensed soda and candy. Rothman reached into his pocket for change.

"Real healthy," Cardello said, walking quickly by the vending machines. Rothman put the coins back in his pocket and followed her.

They rang the bell, and were buzzed into obstetrics. Cardello breathed deeply. "I know that odor. The same disinfectant that Thompson used."

They walked down the narrow corridor, passing pregnant women leaning against the walls, some with small children in their arms and others with older ones sitting at their feet. They passed the nurses' station on the left, the overflowing waiting room on the right, and several smaller examination rooms. The crowd of waiting women in the corridor thinned out as they continued down the hall.

"Sam."

Rothman turned at the sound of his name.

"Angie, hi. What are you doing here? I thought you worked in the emergency room."

"I help out down there when they're swamped. Actually, I'm Dr. Pusitari's nurse. What can I do for you?"

"We have a few questions concerning one of his patients."

"The doctor isn't in right now, but I'd be glad to help you if I can."

"It's in regard to a Miss McGill."

"I read about her in the news. That poor thing. So sad."

"Angie, can you tell us when she had her last appointment?"

"You never heard this from me." Angie motioned them to follow as she led the way to the doctor's office. "She was into the late part of her ninth month. She seemed excited about the baby. Subdued, but excited. Go figure. You never know what a person will do."

She opened the file drawer, and went through it. Then went through it again. "That's strange. Her folder's missing."

Angie leafed through the appointment book on the receptionist's desk. "Monday. This past Monday. She was supposed to come in at three o'clock for her final prenatal visit before her due date."

"And she didn't?"

"No."

Cardello looked at Rothman and raised an eyebrow. "Are you positive, Angie?"

"Absolutely. Dr. Pusitari had three patients due the end of this month, and Ms. McGill was one of them."

The phone rang. "Excuse me." Angie picked it up, and responded, "I can assure you, Mrs. Jones, you won't be having any more internals. You're in your last trimester.… Good, see you later."

This time it was Rothman who looked at Cardello. "Angie, Ms. McGill said she had an internal on Monday morning."

"That would be impossible. First of all, Dr. Pusitari doesn't have morning hours on Mondays. Second, the doctor never examines a patient without me in the room—hospital policy, legal issues and all. And third, he would never perform an internal during a last trimester unless the mother's health was at risk, or the fetus was in distress."

"If I understand what you're saying," Rothman said, referring to the notes he'd been jotting down on his pad, "an internal so late in her pregnancy could have brought on her labor."

"Not could have; would have. Any penetration would have acted upon her cervix to stimulate dilation and uterine contractions, and that would have accelerated her labor."

Rothman gave Cardello an "I told you so" look. "Thanks, Angie."

"If there's anything else I can help you with…"

"You've been very helpful. I'll see you around."

Angie laughed, "Rachel will make sure of that."

Rothman led the way to the hall, but Cardello stopped and turned back. "One more question: does Dr. Pusitari have an associate? Someone who shares the office?"

"No. Just the doctor, me, and the receptionist."

On a hunch, Rothman stopped at the security desk in the main lobby. Chuck turned the sign-in book toward the detectives. "Everyone who comes into this building sign in here?" Rothman asked.

"You betcha," Chuck said.

Chapter 34

Rothman glanced up at the wall clock as he dragged himself through the door into the precinct. He groaned, "only nine-fifteen." He poured a cup of coffee, as Cardello went ahead into their office. She closed her eyes, and randomly grabbed a file from the pile Rothman had left on his desk.

"Okay, what have the gods blessed me with," she asked aloud before looking at it. "Damn. The McGill case. That girl almost had me believing her this morning."

"Teri, maybe she was telling the truth," Rothman said, putting a cup on her desk.

"About the ear, which was conveniently on the early morning news before she left her house? And maybe the rag I found at the creek, with that bit of flesh stuck to it, didn't belong to her, either. But I'd be willing to bet it did." She went to the doorway. "Hey, Lazaro, that report come back yet on the cloth from the creek?"

"The evidence bag you gave me late last night? What d'you think?"

"I want that stat."

"Yeah, yeah. You want everything stat."

Cardello slammed the door.

"Let's see what she was wearing that night." Rothman dialed Dawson's house, then waited until she heard the ringing. He hesitated before putting the phone to his ear.

The housekeeper answered: "Dawson residence."

"Mrs. Rollins, it's Detective Rothman. May I speak to Ms. McGill?"

"Certainly. She's just come in. Child, this call's for you. It's Detective Rothman."

Mallory grabbed the receiver. "You found her. I knew you would. I—"

"No. Not yet. I just need to ask you a question. Did you have a jacket with you on Wednesday night?"

"I had a sweater."

"What color was it?"

"Blue. It was light blue, with dark piping on the collar and cuffs. The buttons were dark blue, too, with ridges around them. I don't know what happened to it."

"Light blue. Dark piping. Buttons with ridges. Thank you, Ms. McGill. We'll be in touch." Rothman slowly lowered the phone.

"I'm sorry, Sam. Judging by her own description, it's her sweater. Blue—knitted, rust-colored stains—we don't need the lab to tell us that's dried blood. Probably wrapped the baby in it and buried it. Dogs found it, and I got all that they left."

"But if she did what you say, do you think she would have given you an accurate description of that sweater? Let's wait for the lab report."

Their door was open, and scuffling sounds in the entrance of the precinct caught Cardello's and Rothman's attention at the same time. They watched from their doorway as a slight black woman dragged a teenager a head taller than her by his ear. She pushed the boy up against the counter.

"You're hurting me. Stop, Ma. Stop."

"You want hurt? I'll give you hurt," the woman punched the boy in the chest. "Now, Leroy, give it to them."

The boy reached into his pocket and pulled out a gun. Immediately, four weapons were drawn and pointing at the boy in response: Sergeant Lazaro's and three other officers' who'd been standing around.

The boy dropped the gun and raised his hands.

"You fools put those things away. You almost gave me a heart attack. My boy here's a good boy. He found that gun." She turned to the boy. "You tell them how it was."

"My ma's right. I was walking under the el and I saw this here gun."

"It just happened to land at your feet. Came out of the sky, maybe," Lazaro said, pulling a plastic bag over his hand before lifting the gun, a Glock 9mm. "A nice choice, compact and light."

"You see, Ma? I told you they wouldn't believe me," the boy said, looking around the room from one officer to another. None of them moved. "Let's get out of here."

"Just a minute." Cardello took a deep breath. "Sam, give me a buck." Rothman pulled some change out of his pocket. "Thanks." Cardello slipped the coins into the soda machine. She pushed the button and grabbed the can of Coke as it came out. "Here," she said, handing it to the boy. "Please come with us." She led the mother and son into the office she and Rothman shared, and closed the door behind them. She motioned for them to sit on the two chairs along the wall, and she sat at her desk. Rothman leaned against his.

"Sorry. You were saying?"

"I picked it up. I was gonna bring it in. You know, for that weapons back money thing. Then I heard they wasn't doing that any more, so I was gonna hock it, but Ma walked into my room. When she saw it, she made me bring it to you."

"I'm glad she did."

"My boy ain't got no record. My boy's a good boy. A Straight A student."

Cardello took the woman's hand. "I'm sure he is. You're doing right by your boy."

"What did you hear, Leroy?"

"Nothin'. I didn't hear nothin'. It was late. Three, maybe four in the morning. I was comin' home."

"What were you doing out so late?"

"My boy works."

"Ma, I can tell them." He turned toward Rothman and sat up straighter. "Got me a summer job. I stock the shelves over at Pathmark. On Atlantic Avenue. It's open 24/7.

"So I got off the Q at Brighton Beach, and I was texting my friend. I dropped my phone, and when I bent down to pick it up, I saw this gun."

"And that's all you saw?"

"No. I looked around. To see was I a mark. Then I saw this guy. At first I thought he was drunk, sort of sitting between the two cars—leaning his head on one. Then I saw blood."

"And what did you do?"

"I slid the gun into my pocket and quick-like, beat it to my house. Fast as I could."

"Without calling to report what you saw?"

"I ain't no fool. I already picked up the gun. It had my prints on it."

"I see," Cardello said, getting up. "I'm going to have to ask you to wait just a bit. We have a few more questions." She walked them over to the holding area, and brought the mother a cup of coffee. "Please wait here. We'll get back to you as soon as possible," she assured the woman.

Cardello ran a check to see if the kid had any previous arrests, while Rothman drove to the Atlantic Avenue Pathmark. An hour later, he was back.

"Teri, the Leroy kid's clean. I checked with the manager, and then ran the surveillance tape. He left at two A.M., like he said."

"No priors, either. I'm running a check on the gun now," Cardello said.

A short time after Leroy and his mother left their office, Lazaro barged into the room.

"This door was closed. This is how you knock on a closed door," Rothman said, knocking on his desk.

"Very funny. Very goddamn funny. You try to help some guys out, and this is what you get."

"OK. What was so Earth-shattering that you couldn't take the time to open a door like a person," Cardello asked.

"Thought you'd want this information for the Brighton Beach John Doe." Lazaro said, tossing the folder onto Rothman's desk. The paper clips Rothman had been lining up with precision flew all over.

"Damn it, Lazaro. Why don't you watch what you're doing?"

"Yeah, yeah. Listen. We had his prints on file. Name's Frank Assanato. Seems he served some time for manslaughter—his nephew's death. Sentence was later commuted. He's been clean for ten years. And there's more."

"We'll read the file. Thank you." Rothman ushered Lazaro to the door. Then he renamed the John Doe file "Frank Assanato," and added it to the three on his desk. He ran his fingers through his hair. "Let's see if we can clear up any of these before we leave tonight."

Cardello picked up the McGill file. "I still think we're going to find this one's open and shut."

"And I still think she's telling the truth," Rothman said. "She could have run, but she didn't."

Cardello shook her head.

"Really. There's something about the girl—"

"Sam, there's something about every pretty girl you deal with."

"No, this is different, Teri. Either she's the worst liar in the world, or she's telling us the truth, and everyone else is lying. Either way, it makes no sense. She's not stupid."

"Oh, come on." Cardello ticked off on her fingers, "She says she had a baby's room ready. You saw her apartment. She says she had an internal Monday. You heard the answering machine. She never even showed for her appointment. She says she called Brad Dawson for a ride. He says no, so she changes her story and says she called the housekeeper. The housekeeper says no. She says someone picked her up, that she didn't drive herself, but we find her car at the creek—and only *her* fingerprints on it. She says she didn't do anything, yet there's blood all over her hands. Everything she's told us has been a lie. And why did she pick the creek? Not a great place for a woman to go alone—unless she had something she wanted to hide. That study from the National Center for Missing and Exploited Children. Kids murdered in the United States? They said mothers who murder their kids usually dump the bodies in womb-like places—water, like a creek."

"And the divers haven't found any sign of the baby in that creek," Rothman reminded her. "They also said mothers who murder their kids tend to be schizophrenic. She's not. So what was her motive?"

"Maybe she thought she was sparing the kid some kind of suffering. Remember, the baby's father died a few months back, a gas explosion? That would be enough reason."

"Look, if you want to beat a dead horse, go right ahead, but I've got some hard-earned vacation time coming to me. I'm taking Nadine and Sammy out to East Hampton. I'm going to enjoy myself this weekend."

Rothman sat down and put his head in his hands. "Teri, when she talked about getting ready for that kid, she came alive. I think she wanted it. And at the hospital, didn't Angie say she couldn't wait to have her baby?"

"But Angie also said she didn't show for her appointment." Cardello touched his shoulder. "Sam, I know you once made a mistake."

"A mistake? Is that what you call it? I let them convict that man. Wrongly. He said he was innocent, and I didn't dig deep enough to prove it."

"And you also didn't put a gun to that poor bastard's head. He did that on his own."

"Well what if she *is* telling the truth? The divers didn't come up with anything."

Exasperated, Cardello's voice went up. She threw her hands up in the air. "Because she buried it."

"We won't know that until the lab report is in. Teri, maybe we're missing something in her apartment."

"All right, if it will make you feel better, we'll go back there one more time."

Chapter 35

Rothman pulled up to the curb. A throng of reporters and cameramen were being held back from the courtyard by several sawhorses and officers.

"Looks like the media has already convicted the girl," Rothman said, as he and Cardello pushed aside the mikes stuck in their faces, and shielded their eyes from the flashing cameras.

The blind man was sitting at the window, leaning on the sill, his position identical to that of the day before. And the super's little boy was still playing with the Jack-in-the-Box.

"Howdy, detectives. Back so soon?"

"Mr. Lowenthal, right?"

"Last time I checked, that was my name."

"Anything out of the ordinary going on around here lately?"

"Are you blind, too? Those newsmen." He nodded toward the street. "Lots of commotion out there today. They've been all over the building. The super had to call the cops."

"Must be driving everyone nuts."

"Nah. But that kid is driving me nuts. For the last two days, he hasn't stopped cranking that damned toy."

"Two days?"

"That's when that infernal noise first started."

Cardello walked over to the child, and sat down beside him.

"That's a nice toy. Where did you get it?"

The little boy held it tightly to himself. "I didn't steal it. Honest. My Papa found it in the 'cinerator room. He gave it to me."

Rothman came closer to the window. "When's bulk pick-up, Mr. Lowenthal?"

"Was. Late Wednesday afternoon. If you ask me, you're barking up the wrong tree. Ms. McGill wouldn't hurt a fly."

Carrying a six-foot ladder, Willie Williams tried to maneuver through the front door. Rothman hurried over to hold the door open for him. "Back to take another look at McGill's place?"

Rothman nodded.

Willie, not too friendly this time, leaned the ladder against the wall, shifted the tool belt on his shoulder, and pulled out his key ring.

"Elevator's still out," he said, as he took the key labeled 5B off the ring. "Return it when you come down."

"What exactly are we looking for," Cardello asked, as she trudged up the five flights of stairs behind Rothman.

"I'm not sure, but let's knock on some doors. With ten apartments on this floor, someone is bound to know something." No one answered at 5C, nor at 5D. At 5E, a Polish woman came to the door. She spoke no English. When they knocked on the door across the hall, Mrs. Russo opened it as much as the chain would allow: about four inches.

"We're inquiring about your neighbor, Mallory McGill."

"Nice girl—until she took up with the likes of…" she lowered her voice and whispered, "…a colored man."

"Oh?"

"Saw him beating her up in the hall yesterday. Poor thing was crying her heart out."

Just then, a middle-aged woman—arms loaded with Stop and Shop grocery bags—came out of the stairwell huffing and puffing. "Damn elevators. They're out of service more than they're in."

"Here, let me give you a hand," Rothman said, taking the bags from the woman.

"Why, you're a real Sir Lancelot. Thank you."

"We're inquiring about the woman in 5B."

"Mallory McGill? I know her. A sweet girl. Can't believe what the papers are saying. I saw the baby's layette." She shuffled through her purse until she found her keys. "She hung my towel rack when it fell off. If I called the super, I'd still be waiting. The older tenants keep him busy, day and night."

The woman opened her door, then took her groceries from Rothman. "Wouldn't pay to knock on any of the other doors. The tenants in those apartments only speak Russian, Chinese, and Polish," she said, pointing.

"Thank you. You've been most helpful."

* * *

Rothman opened the door to the McGill apartment. "Let's go through her papers. There might be something we missed. Something to substantiate her story."

Rothman leafed through a pile of Mallory's sketches, while Cardello went through the bureau drawers. One particular sketch caught his eye, and he held it up for Cardello to see. "This kid. He's the one they call the Judge. He told us he didn't know where Eduardo lived, but we saw him coming out of the alley."

"And don't forget, he was at the rooming house when the woman was fried."

"A person of interest?"

"Could be… that Mrs. Russo said McGill had taken up with a black man." Cardello pulled out a leather folder labeled "Important" from the bottom bureau drawer. A photograph fell from the folder to the floor. It was a shot of Mallory and a man who looked like Brad. Cardello picked it up and studied it closely. In the picture, Mallory was carrying a small bouquet of flowers in one hand, and holding her other hand toward the camera. "Hey, I might have something here. A wedding band."

She turned the photo over. "It's dated November—this was taken nine months ago."

"So she was married?"

"If she was, inheritance might have been a motive. The dead brother's child would have stood to inherit…"

"And Uncle Brad's share would have been cut."

Rothman rolled up the drawing of Moses, and knocked on Mrs. Russo's door again.

"Yes?" Mrs. Russo asked through the slit the chain allowed.

Rothman unfurled the photo. "Could you tell me if this is the man you saw in the hall with Ms. McGill?"

The door closed, the chain rattled, and Mrs. Russo opened the door. She grabbed the drawing. "That's him. I'd know him anywhere. I came out and chased him away." Cardello and Rothman exchanged looks that went unnoticed by the woman as she prattled on about the changing neighborhood.

Rothman knocked on the grocery woman's door. "Excuse me for bothering you again, but do you know this man?"

"I've seen him leaving Mallory's apartment."

"Did you ever hear them fighting?"

"Absolutely not."

"We heard she was having a rocky relationship with—"

"You've probably been talking to Mrs. Russo." She smiled at the old woman standing in the hall, then whispered, "She's getting more batty every day. Makes up stories all the time. You can't believe a word she says."

Willie was just coming out of an apartment on the first floor, unbuckling his tool belt, when Cardello and Rothman came down the stairs. "Building maintenance. Someone's always got something for me to fix." He shifted his tools, and took the key that Rothman held out.

"Any personal jobs for the tenants here?"

"Some. But never during work hours. On my own time. None of that double dipping stuff for me. I've got a wife and four babies—with another one on the way." His chest puffed up proudly.

"Did Ms. McGill ever ask you to do any work for her?"

"No. That woman's very self reliant. Pity what happened to her baby. Can't figure why those blood suckers," he nodded toward the media, "are here."

"Oh?"

"Yeah. She miscarried. Plain and simple. Almost cracked up over it. I hear she's taking it pretty hard."

"How'd you hear?"

"Her aunt came by. She asked me to get rid of everything that would remind Ms. McGill of her baby."

"Did you get her name," Cardello asked.

"No."

"How'd you know it was her aunt?"

"She told me. Had Ms. McGill's key. Knew about the baby."

"What did she look like?"

"Hard to tell. She was an old woman. Really bent over. Had sort of a hump on her back. Made her walk with her head stuck forward— reminded me of a turtle."

"Her hair color? Her face?"

"Grey hair. She had grey hair. But I couldn't see much of her face. She was wearing dark glasses. Said she was a mess from all the crying over the baby."

"Anything else you can tell us about her?"

"She had sort of a musty smell, like a lot of old people have."

"What about her paints?" Cardello asked.

"Pardon, ma'am?"

"Ms. McGill's paints. Did you touch them?"

"The aunt told me to move them into the bedroom—to make it a studio. Then she cleaned the apartment. Was still at it when I left."

"We'll need that key again." Rothman said.

He hurried back up the stairs, with Cardello right behind him. "Sam, just remember, having a room for her baby doesn't prove she didn't do away with it."

"Yeah, yeah." Rothman opened the door, and they went to the living room. "You do the honors, Teri."

Cardello kneeled down beside the too-small area rug, and lifted the edge. The floor beneath the rug had been scrubbed so clean, it was lighter than the floor around it. She ran a fingernail between the slats. Blue paint stuck to her nail.

Chapter 36

As soon as Mrs. Rollins left with her shopping list, Mallory returned to Brad's study. She was searching through every file for the ones that said OBT when the front door bell rang. Nervously, she inched the curtain aside and peered out of the window. All day yesterday, news trucks and reporters had been camped on Brad's lawn and at her apartment. She'd had to park Keith's car in the street around the corner, and crawl through the backyard hedges. Relieved now to see Detectives Rothman and Cardello, and not the reporters who had been hounding her, she hurried to the front door and opened it.

"Do you have any word for me," she asked hopefully.

"Nothing yet. Just a few more questions. Is there some place we can talk?"

Dejected, Mallory led the way to the living room, and sat down.

"Ms. McGill, were you and Keith Dawson married," Rothman asked, as he sat opposite her.

"Yes. We were."

Cardello glanced at Rothman. "And you kept it a secret because…"

"Because of his grandfather."

"So the old man disapproved?"

"No. That wasn't it at all. Keith was, he…" Mallory stopped.

"Please, Ms. McGill. Please cooperate."

"Cooperate?" Mallory's voice shot up. "Someone took my baby. She's gone. You should be out looking for her, and you're asking *me* to cooperate? Why should I? You don't believe a word I say."

"Mallory, please. We really are trying to help," Cardello said, leading her back to the chair she had vacated.

Mallory looked from one detective to the other. "This is the last time."

Cardello nodded.

"Keith was so happy when the doctor told us I was pregnant. He said, let's get married. And that very same day, we went for our marriage license. The following day, we were married in a civil ceremony at Borough Hall."

Mallory looked into Detective Cardello's eyes. "I told you. All I dreamed about was being married and having a family of my own."

"Then why the secret? Help us to understand," Cardello said.

"Right after the ceremony, we went to tell Keith's grandfather. We were going to tell his brother Brad, and Mrs. Rollins, who had practically raised the brothers, too."

"And what stopped you?"

"We didn't get a chance. We told them about the baby first."

"And their reactions?"

"The Grandfather was overjoyed. Brad seemed happy."

"And the housekeeper?"

"She didn't react the way I thought she would. She was never demonstrative. Now that I think about it, she did seem a bit unsettled. I'm sure it was because she resented having to do so much in such a short time."

"Keith's grandfather began making wedding plans immediately. He had his heart set on a large affair in the back yard. He said, 'June. Four months. That should be enough time to prepare, and the garden will be blooming.' He told Mrs. Rollins she'd be in charge of the food. He talked about her ordering canopies for the sun, and finding a band, and... I swear, he had more energy than he'd had in months."

"So you never told the family you had gotten married?"

"No. Keith and I looked at each other. He shrugged. I slipped my wedding ring off my finger and into my pocket."

"And after Keith died?"

"Then there didn't seem to be much point in saying anything."

"But wouldn't your baby have stood to inherit?"

"I guess. But Keith was killed. I was shaken. Nothing mattered after that."

"Tell us about the accident."

"We had just moved into our new home in the Slope. The police said it was a faulty gas pipe that caused the explosion. Keith was gone, the brownstone totaled."

"Where were you when that happened?"

"In my apartment, on East 17th Street."

Detective Cardello raised her eyebrows. "You said you'd moved into your new home."

"We did. But the top floor was being renovated: skylights and large windows, northern and southern exposures. It was going to be the most perfect studio. Until it was ready, I continued to work in my old apartment. That's what saved me. I had a commissioned piece I needed to finish, and had gone back there to work on it that evening."

"And after that?"

"Everything was a blur. I stayed in The Grandfather's house, and Brad made all of the arrangements. I got through the funeral in a daze. Many well-wishers came, so I wouldn't be alone, when all I wanted was to be alone."

"Brad held me together when I was falling apart." Mallory sighed. "He was so kind. So much like Keith, but now… he's changed. I feel more alone than I ever did before."

"And why do you think he's changed?"

"I don't know. The baby. It was after he brought me here… almost as soon as he brought me here. He became different. Angry. He blames me for everything that happened."

"Mallory, do you have your marriage certificate?"

"Yes. I keep it in the bottom drawer of my bureau. In a folder with all of my important papers."

Rothman and Cardello glanced at each other.

"Does anyone else have access to your apartment?"

"Brad has a spare set of keys."

"Thank you for your cooperation, Miss McGill. We'll be in touch." The detectives turned to leave.

"Oh, one more thing," Cardello said, "Do you have any family: cousins, uncles, aunts?"

"There's no one. It was just my mother and me."

"No aunt?"

"No."

Mallory watched the detectives walk toward their car. She had almost told them about the files she'd found, but what could she say? There was an address of an abandoned house? Why would they listen to her now? They hadn't believed her before.

She went back to Brad's office, and sat in the high-backed leather chair. "I have to think," she said. "I'm a smart woman. I can figure this out myself. There has to be an answer. There's an answer to everything. I just need to find an ally. Someone who will believe me."

Jostled from foster home to foster home, Mallory had never developed a knack for making friends. And then, her art had been enough company for her. She'd always been so involved with her painting that she'd had little need for people in her life—until she'd met Keith. Then Brad, and their grandfather, and even the housekeeper had become sort of family to her. And there was also Moses. Now Keith and The Grandfather were gone, and Brad had distanced himself from her. But she had Moses. She smiled when she thought of him. He was like the kid brother she'd never had.

She dialed him, but he didn't pick up. After several attempts, she left a message on his cell phone. "I'll wait for ten minutes. Then, if I don't hear from you, I'm going myself. I think I found the place."

Chapter 37

"It's hot as hell, and not even ten yet," Rothman said, pulling a crumpled handkerchief out of his back pocket and wiping his brow. "I don't know how you can wear that damned jacket of yours. I need a cold drink." Rothman and Cardello stopped at Rachel's for the second time that day.

"She did have that file in the bottom drawer," Rothman said, helping himself to a bottle of iced tea from the cooler. He hit the bottom of the bottle with the palm of his hand, then opened the lid.

"But no marriage license," Cardello said, taking a Dove bar from the next cooler.

"What do you make of the aunt thing the super told us about?"

"Beats me."

"McGill was right about the blue paint."

The bell over the door tinkled, and a teenager walked in. The detectives looked up briefly, then went back to their conversation.

"Hi, Dirk. How's your mom?" Rachel asked from behind the counter.

"She's real good, Ms. Rachel. She appreciated you running an account for us while she was sick. Anyway, I come to pay you back." Dirk pulled out a roll of bills, and peeled off three twenties. He held the money, looking at it for a bit, and then, reluctantly, handed it over.

"These are twenties. Where'd you get these? You do something wrong and your mama will skin you alive. She doesn't need you back in jail. You hear me?"

"Yes, ma'am. I hear you. I didn't do nothing wrong. I earned it. A lady gave it to me to drive her car. Honest. A sweet little yellow VW."

Rothman and Cardello's heads both popped up. "Hey, kid, come over here."

Dirk lunged for the door, but Rothman grabbed him. "I'm not going to hurt you… if you're straight with me. Tell me about this lady."

"I wasn't doing nothing. Just hanging out."

"I don't care if you were standing on your head and pissing wooden nickels. Tell me," Rothman said, pushing Dirk onto the stool he'd just vacated.

"This lady, she picks me up on Surf and Stillwell." Dirk looked toward Cardello, then turned back to Rothman, and lowered his voice. "She don't want my regular kind of services. I tell her I don't want no trouble. I just got back from juvie. She tells me it's not like that. She's only interested could I drive a car. I tell her yeah. So she says she just wants me to drive her sister's car home, and don't tell no one, because her sister was drunk. She drives me to somewhere in Midwood and stops at the VW. She says 'here, put these on,' and hands me a pair of rubber gloves. Her sister's real particular about her car, she says. Then she gives me the keys, and I follow her to Bayview Avenue."

"That's near Coney Island Creek?" Cardello asks, writing down everything Dirk says.

"Yeah. She says to leave the key under the mat, and she drives me back to Surf, and gives me a hundred bucks."

"What did the lady look like? How old do you think she was?"

Dirk shrugged. "I couldn't tell. These white bitches, they all look alike."

"Oh, come on. What color was her hair?"

"She was wearing one of those turban things, like the sisters wear. Couldn't see her hair."

"The turban thing. Was it like a scarf?"

"Sort of. And she had these gigantic sunglasses on, like she was some kind of movie star."

Cardello turned to Rothman, "Huge, dark glasses. Like the old aunt."

Rothman nodded. "Dirk, was she hunched over?"

"Naah. She was a tall broad."

Chapter 38

While waiting for Moses to call her back, Mallory had curled up in Brad's club chair and fallen asleep. It was nearly noon when she woke.

She pulled her cell phone out of her skirt pocket. "Be there, Moses. Please be there. Pick up. Come on," she said as she dialed him again. Nothing. Her battery had gone dead. There was no phone in her room, so she lifted Brad's phone from its cradle. But before she could click to get a dial tone, she heard a male voice. Covering the mouthpiece with one hand, she put the phone to her ear.

"I'm telling you, I saw her looking around."

The voice sounded familiar. But from where? Where had she heard it before?

"Look, taking a kid from a woman who wants an abortion is one thing, but doing an abortion on a woman who wants her kid is another story."

Mallory pressed her hand tightly over her mouth as she gasped. The word "abortion" cut through her as surely as if it had been a sword. As surely as if someone had ripped her open and pulled out her insides. She grabbed her stomach and lowered herself into Brad's chair, the phone pressed against her. Slowly, she brought it up to the cradle, but as she did, she heard the other person yelling, "Cut the crap. We both know you sold the kid."

"Sold the kid." That's what he said. She heard him say it: "Sold the kid." All she could process was that her baby was alive. And that was enough. She leaned back in the chair, staring blankly at the phone in her hand.

She jerked upright. The caller: he had to be in the house with her. She ran out of Brad's office and up the stairs, the thumping of her sneakered feet muted by the thick carpet. One by one, she opened each of the doors on the second floor. There was no one there. She made a mad dash for the kitchen. Mrs. Rollins had returned from the green grocers, and, with her back to Mallory, was basting a chicken. There was no sign of shopping bags. The woman had already put the vegetables in the refrigerator and the fruit in its crystal bowl.

"Who's in the house?"

"Why just you and me. Mr. B's gone out."

"No. There's someone else in here. A man."

Mrs. Rollins wiped her hands on her dishtowel, and turned to Mallory. "A man?"

"I heard him on the phone. Quick, call the police."

"What are you talking about, child? You're imagining things again." The housekeeper pulled out a chair. "Come sit down. I'll make you a cup of tea."

"No. We've got to find him. He knows about my baby."

"Who knows? Listen to yourself. You're not making any sense."

Mallory paced the floor. "He sold my baby. The man. Not the one in the house. The other man. The one on the phone."

"I thought you said a man in the house was on the phone."

"He was. They were. They were talking to each other. I'm going to call the detectives."

"Ms. McGill, will you listen to yourself? You're sounding crazy. They'll be coming here on a wild goose chase. How do you ever expect them to do their jobs if you bother them with such nonsense? I'll tell you what: have a nice cup of tea, and after I get the chicken basted, I'll go look with you."

"No. I'm calling them now."

Rothman rested his finger on the doorbell to Dawson's house, as he surveyed the army of reporters milling around. "These guys don't give up."

"I can't blame them. All of a sudden, the girl's memory is back? Should be interesting to see how the rest of the day unfolds." Cardello counted off on her fingers: "There was the guy with the missing ear under the el. Then the hospital. Then the girl's apartment for the *second* time, and then back here *again*. "What was it? Two hours ago we were here? And it isn't even lunch time yet."

Mallory hurried to the door and opened it wide, not caring that the reporters' flashes were going off in her face. She pulled the detectives in and slammed the door shut. "There's a man in the house. You've got to find him. Hurry. He knows about my baby."

Mrs. Rollins came from the kitchen wiping her hands on her apron. "Ms. McGill is sure she heard two men talking on the phone, and Mr. B isn't here." She looked at the detectives, and shook her head. Mallory caught her motion from the corner of her eye.

"They weren't just talking. They were talking about my baby." She looked from Mrs. Rollins to the detectives. "Please, you've got to believe me."

"We'll look around, if it will make you feel more comfortable."

"Suit yourselves," Mrs. Rollins said, throwing up her hands. "But the doors and windows have been locked all morning, except when I brought the groceries in. Air conditioning, you know." She turned toward the kitchen. "I would have known if anyone was here."

"I was in Brad's office when I heard the conversation." At the mention of Brad's office, Mrs. Rollins stopped walking. Mallory saw the look of displeasure on the housekeeper's face as she turned toward her, but she didn't care. She didn't care about anything except finding her baby.

"So we can rule out the office." Cardello drew her gun. "I'll look down here. You take the second floor."

Rothman went through each room, looking behind doors, under beds, in closets, armoires, and in bathrooms.

"Sorry, Ms. McGill, but there is no one here," Detective Rothman said.

"There has to be. I know what I heard. Someone has to believe me."

"We'll see ourselves out, Mrs. Rollins. I think you'd better stay with Ms. McGill."

Chapter 39

Mallory stood at the door, watching as Mrs. Rollins saw the detectives out.

"They think I'm crazy. Don't they? Maybe I am. Mrs. Rollins, what about you? Do you think I'm crazy, too?"

The housekeeper led Mallory to the sofa in the living room. "You've had a bad shock. Your mind is playing tricks on you, that's all."

"I can't allow my mind to wander. I must focus on my baby."

"Oh, child, when will it register? Your baby is gone. You'll never hold her. Go ahead and grieve."

"No. I have to wait."

"Wait for what?"

Mallory's body, overcome with exhaustion, sunk back into the couch. Mrs. Rollins offered her a pill.

A pill? Mallory's mind came alive. Brad had told her that he knew nothing of the pills Mrs. Rollins was giving her. If he was telling the truth, why would Mrs. Rollins want her sedated? What did she have to gain?

Mallory took the pill. Only she slipped it into her pocket instead of her mouth. Maybe if she faked sleep, she might discover something. A few minutes later, as she pretended to doze, Mrs. Rollins went to Brad's office. From where she sat, Mallory couldn't see into the office, but she heard the file cabinets opening and closing.

A short time later, Mrs. Rollins returned to the living room. At the baby grand piano, she picked up a heart-shaped silver frame. Gently, she touched the image in it.

Mallory knew which photograph Mrs. Rollins was looking at, because of its frame. It was the one she'd copied for The Grandfather: two-year-old Brad with a radiant smile. The Grandfather had loved the painting, and hung it in his study. Then, yesterday, when she'd gone looking for clothes, Mallory had seen it in Mrs. Rollins' sewing room. The woman held it away from her. "You had your chance. But you're no better than the old man. I went to your grandfather. I had no money, no job, nothing but a bulging belly. I pleaded with him to help me," she said to the picture.

Some of the pieces came together for Mallory. "You're Brad's mother. He was the child you abandoned," she said, getting to her feet.

"I... I..." The picture fell from Mrs. Rollins' hands, hitting several keys on the piano, the noise loud in the still house. "You startled me. I thought you were sleeping," she said quickly, returning the picture to the piano lid.

"I'm right, aren't I?"

"No. Of course not. You don't know what you're talking about. You haven't been well." She picked up another picture and furiously dusted it, and then another after that.

Mallory grabbed Mrs. Rollins and shook her. "What's this all about?" Then she shook her harder, "Tell me. Tell me!"

"I promised The Grandfather I'd never tell. That was our agreement when he let me come back."

"But The Grandfather's gone now. Does Brad know?"

"Mr. B... Oh, Ms. McGill, I don't know what to do," Mrs. Rollins began to sob. She twisted her handkerchief in her hands."I shouldn't tell you. Mr. B made me promise not to, but…" in a rush of words almost too quick to follow, Mrs. Rollins blurted out, "Mr. B has your baby."

Before the words could register with Mallory, the housekeeper pulled out a slip of paper and wrote an address. "Here. Go quickly. You may be in time…"

Mallory looked at the address. Her eyes widened. "I know that house."

"Go back there now. Wait for him if he isn't there. He has your baby."

Chapter 40

Cardello straightened the files on her desk. "After our shift, I'm heading home. Going to get my family, and we're off for the weekend. Sure you don't want to join us? Your godson misses you."

"Nah," Rothman said, enjoying a cup of coffee. He munched on a jelly doughnut as he realigned the paper clips spread across his desk. "Thanks for the offer, but Sammy's got friends out there, and you ladies will have a better time without me."

Cardello picked up a folder and spread the photographs.

Rothman leaned across his desk to see them. "Gonzalez, the kid they found in the lot in Coney Island? The overdose." Crumbs fell from his mouth onto the morgue shots. His coffee sloshed over the photos.

"Hey, watch out. Have a little respect for the dead." Cardello mopped up the spill, and stuffed the photos back into the file. She pulled out the McGill file next.

"Teri, the kid's story about the yellow car changes things, don't you think?"

"Who knows? We still need to find a person with a motive."

Rothman picked up the latest file, the one Lazaro had barged in and thrown onto his desk before they'd gone off to check McGill's apartment for the second time. "Frank Assanato. Poor bastard. Yada, yada, yada," he read, skimming the contents.

"Holy crap." He pulled the pages closer and bolted upright in his chair. "Will you look at this."

"What?" Cardello asked, gathering her things, determined to get home while Nadine was still talking to her, so their weekend away wouldn't be ruined.

"The key case they found on him… It had a slip of paper in it, with an address that matched the address of the Park Slope gas explosion seven months ago. Brad Dawson's brother, Keith."

Cardello stopped what she was doing. "I think Dawson just became more than a person of interest."

"Wait," Rothman said. "There's more. According to the lab, the white powder they found on the vic's sneakers…"

"Yes?"

"Baby formula."

Cardello jumped up, and grabbed the file from Rothman's hands. She rifled through the papers. "There's no location." She opened the door, and called to the Sergeant. "Lazaro, where the hell did this guy live?"

"Couldn't find an address. We're trying to reach his next of kin now. A sister."

"I want that stat. High priority."

"Yeah, yeah," Lazaro said, banging his empty lunch box loudly on the counter. "I'm on it."

"Sam, that girl was right all along, and now she's in friggin' danger," Cardello said, rifling her center drawer for a piece of gum. She pulled out each of her side drawers in turn. "Damn, I'm out."

"Good. Maybe now you'll stop chewing that crap," Rothman said.

"I think better when I'm chewing." Her jacket was hanging behind the door, near Rothman's desk. She got up and tore through her pockets. She pulled out a package of Trident. A fabric scrap came out with the gum, and fell to Rothman's desk.

"Colorful, isn't it," he said, picking it up.

Cardello took the piece of cloth from him, and studied it. "Son of a… the retarded girl, Dora. She gave that to me." She opened the door, and called to the Sergeant. "Have someone bring me the evidence bags from the McGill case and make that—"

"Yeah, I know: stat."

Rothman and Cardello spread Mallory's dress on the desk. Between the crusted dirt, dried blood turned brown, and blue paint, bits of turquoise and green fabric, and the flawless hand-stitching of the original garment showed through. And where a pocket had been ripped away, a large patch of the true colors were visible.

Cardello placed the material scrap that Dora had given her on the clothing where the pocket had been, positioning it until the pattern aligned. "Well, what do you know? A perfect match."

"So where do you think the girl picked it up?"

"We couldn't get any information from her if we tried. But her old man said she never wandered far off, so my guess is, right on her street."

"I'll drive," Rothman said. He grabbed the car keys off their hook, and ran to the car, doughnut in hand. Cardello, right behind him, had barely pulled her door shut when he floored the gas pedal and shot out into traffic. As anxious to get back to Elgart Street as he was, his driving like bat out of hell didn't annoy her today. Quickly, she buckled her seat belt.

"Sam, I've been thinking about that landlord."

Rothman shoved the rest of the doughnut into his mouth. The tires squealed as he turned sharply and rounded the corner onto Surf Avenue.

Cardello seized the overhead grab handle, and held on tight.

The one in the house next to the Dora girl's?"

"Yes. That Willard Thompson. I can't put my finger on it, but something's been bothering me about him."

"Darn," Sam said, licking his fingers. "I got jelly all over my hand."

"That's it. His hand! My father was a mechanic. I used to watch him wash his hands. As much as he scrubbed, he could never get all of the grease washed out of the crevices and out from under his finger nails. His hands always looked dirty. And they were rough. That guy's hands were soft, and immaculate. So why did he tell us he was a mechanic? And why were his windows boarded up? What was in his place?"

"You've got something there. I was just thinking about his hesitation when he saw us coming. Like he was scared."

"I caught that, too. And he said the hall smelled from disinfectant. But it was filthy. I guess it wouldn't hurt to pay him another visit."

"With the retarded girl now in the hands of Child Protective Services, and her father in jail, the only house occupied in that row of dilapidated old buildings is Willard Thompson's." Cardello walked through the alley to his yard. She tried his doors, front and side. "Locked."

"And with no probable cause, requesting a search warrant would be useless," Rothman said.

"Then let's find one." Cardello walked slowly up the street, studying every inch of the sidewalk, from the broken stair railings to the dead shrubs. Rothman, beside her, kept his eyes on the trash and dirt at the curb. Together, they checked each house. Other than using a crowbar or a pickax, there was no way anyone could get into any of them. They checked the rusted cyclone fences that backed the yards and the lot, scrutinizing every bit of paper that had blown into them and stuck there over the years. Rothman picked up a broken curtain rod, and turned over all of the dirt that had accumulated on the concrete around the foundations. Cardello turned over each bit of trash on the ground.

Chapter 41

Moses couldn't be sure how much time had passed as he lay on the floor of Thompson's apartment, but when he opened his eyes, his head had stopped spinning. Only now it was ringing. Then he realized it wasn't his head that was ringing; he was hearing the cell phone Thompson had dropped. Luckily, it had landed face up, and it was one of those that didn't open and close. He squirmed over to it and pecked at it with his nose, until he finally hit the green button.

"Answer me, damn you," came the gravelly voice. "I know you're there. You can't get away from me. Your nice friend Vickie left your new cell phone number on her bulletin board before she, uh, met with a little accident, so you'd better be listening. McGill's on her way over. You've got to get rid of her. She knows too much."

Moses' eyes opened wide. He tried to talk, but the best he could do with his mouth taped shut was hum like a kazoo.

"Shut up and listen." The voice grew even more shrill. "I'm coming over to make sure you do it."

Moses had to get out. He had to find Mallory. His eye caught the scalpel he'd threatened Thompson with. It was on the floor, near the surgical table. He turned away, and reached behind himself with the tips of his fingers, but it slid from his grasp, under the table, and out of his reach. Lying on his arms, he shoved the table, but the only thing that moved was him. He rolled over and over until he reached the table beside the cot. With his ankles bound, he kicked over the table. The lamp on it smashed to the floor. Its glass base shattered, and he was thrust into darkness.

He squirmed around, jabbing the tips of his fingers again and again as he felt for a piece of the glass to free himself. Finally, he managed to grab a piece between his fingers. He arched his back, and bent his bound legs back until they connected with the glass in his hands. He jabbed at the tape between his ankles. Only the tape covering his mouth prevented him from screaming as the glass cut into him. Finally, the tape gave way, and his legs were free. He moved them until he felt the circulation coming back, then he propelled himself to the surgical table. With his back to it, he pushed up until he was standing.

Outside, Rothman hit the door with the rod again and again. "Damn it. Looks like a dead end."

Moses heard the banging. He had to get the attention of whoever was outside. He kicked at the metal table. He knocked over a chair. He tried to scream, but all that came out of his taped mouth was "Mmmm, mmmm."

Cardello, standing next to the steps, and equally as frustrated as Rothman, kicked the last bit of trash with the toe of her leather shoe. A glint of something shiny caught her eye. She squatted down near the steps, and sifted the dry dirt through her fingers until she found a small gold disk. As she brushed off the dirt, an artist's palette etched in the metal became visible.

She held it up for Rothman to see.

"I'd say you just found probable cause." He flipped open his cell phone to call for a search warrant. Then he snapped it closed and looked at Cardello. "I think I heard someone scream."

"Me, too." She grinned. "If someone's life is in danger…"

"The hell with the warrant."

Rothman dashed to the car, and returned with the crowbar.

Using his hands, still bound behind him, Moses felt his way over to the counter. He pulled a drawer open. It crashed to the floor, spilling silverware all over. On his knees now, he felt around in the dark until he found a paring knife. He maneuvered it into position between his fingers, and with the slight motion the tape allowed him, sawed at the tape until it ripped and his hands were free. Then he yanked the tape that covered his mouth. He was about to call out when his street smarts kicked in. He'd wait and see.

He heard noises as Rothman forced one padlock open and then another until all three were hanging to one side. Recognizing the detectives' voices as they jimmied the door, he made his way back to the small room, and crawled back behind the leaning mattress.

To Moses, the hinges' slight squeak as the door opened sounded like nails across a chalk board. Cardello drew her flashlight out of her belt. Its beam of light washed over the table and stopped at the stirrups at the end. Cardello lifted one. "A nice touch. Belongs in a gynecologist's office, not a kitchen." The beam then traveled to the floor. Blood glistened in its light. She nodded to Rothman, and they both drew their guns. Droplets of blood led toward the door Moses had just closed. Rothman stood, his gun ready. Cardello kicked it open.

"Don't shoot. I'm coming out," Moses said, as he crawled out from under the mattress and raised his hands.

"You again. What are you, Houdini or something? You're everywhere. Like stepping into dog shit wherever I go. How did you get in here?"

Cardello flipped on the overhead light, as Rothman reached out to grab Moses' arm.

"Damn it, kid. What happened to you," he asked, stepping back as he saw the blood on Moses for the first time.

"That don't matter. Ms. McGill's in trouble. Bad trouble. She's gonna be killed."

"Yeah, kid. Sure. And that's why you were hiding under a mattress— to protect her."

"No. It's the truth. It has to do with Mr. Dawson, a guy called Dantano, and the guy who lives here. He knocked me out. I don't know how long ago. Look." Moses touched his cheek, raw from where he'd pulled off the tape. He grabbed the detective's sleeve. "Really. You've got to believe me."

Rothman pulled his arm away. "And I should believe you because…"

"I heard him on the phone. I was hiding behind that." Moses nodded toward the mattress resting against the wall. "He took a wad of money out of here." Moses ripped at the floor boards Thompson had replaced. They wouldn't budge. "Here's where I hit my head when he pushed me," he said, grabbing Cardello's hand and bringing it to the growing lump at the back of his head. He winced. "I'm telling the truth. He's on his way to Alaska. Please. You've got to help her." He was near to tears. "She's my friend."

Cardello watched Moses as she picked up her phone. "Check Kennedy Airport for any flights to Alaska. If there are none, check LaGuardia. We're looking for—"

"—a white guy. Old. Tall. Bald, but with a grey beard," Moses finished.

"Matches our landlord," Rothman said.

"What else?"

"He was wearing a navy suit with a white shirt, and his bag was brown with two straps that buckled. The size you can take on a plane with you, like carry-on."

"Please, he wants to have Ms. McG killed."

"Who's this *he*?"

"The guy on the phone. He was real loud. He had sort of a raspy voice. I heard the whole conversation. He said, 'You've got to get rid of her. She knows too much.'"

Moses looked from Rothman's stone-like face to Cardello's more open gaze.

"Miss, please. I never begged no one before, but you gotta believe me now."

Cardello lifted Moses' chin, and looked directly into his pleading eyes. "Okay. Let's get over to Dawson's, quick. We'll call a squad car to get you to the hospital on the way, to take care of your legs and hands."

"Let's just hurry. Ms. McGill, she's in real trouble."

They didn't have to make the call. A patrol car pulled up to the curb as they left Thompson's apartment. "Hey Sam, Teri. What's going on?"

Rothman walked over to the blue and white car, and looked into the window. "Hey Paulie, how you doing? How come they got you out of your unmarked?"

"Just cruising. With homicides growing the mayor's going ballistic.

"Oh yeah, I heard. He wants visibility on the streets." Nodding toward Moses, who was out of earshot, Rothman said, "do me a favor. That kid's all cut up. Get him over to the emergency room, but don't let him out of your sight. When he's patched up, bring him over to the precinct. He may be looking at some serious time."

The officer got out of the car to escort Moses.

Moses turned to Cardello. "You gotta find her."

"We will. The officer will get you to the emergency room. We'll connect later," Rothman said in his most soothing voice. No sense alerting the kid that his basketball had given him away.

Chapter 42

It was right after Mrs. Rollins watched Mallory pass through the hedge that she called Thompson. She grabbed her bag, and put her hat on her head, as the doorbell rang. Whoever was ringing had his finger pressed on the bell, and the chime played over and over. She opened the door, her look of annoyance obvious to the detectives. "Yes? What is it now? I was just going out." She pushed a stray hair behind her ear. Her hat sat askew on her head.

"Please call Ms. McGill."

"I'm sorry, Detective Rothman, but she isn't here."

Rothman had jumped out of the car and run to the front steps before Cardello parked. Now she caught up to him, as he was saying, "What do you mean she's not here?"

"Excuse me, may I use your powder room," Cardello interrupted. Then, without waiting for an answer, she hurried past the housekeeper, and into the house.

"Where did Ms. McGill go?" Rothman's voice was rising.

"I don't know." The old woman looked after Cardello, who was running toward the kitchen.

"Mrs. Rollins, I'm speaking to you," Rothman said.

The housekeeper turned her attention back to him. Rothman couldn't make out if she sounded more inconvenienced or anxious when she answered, "Ms. McGill ran out right after you left this morning. Said she didn't want to deal with all of this any more. That poor child was talking nonsense. She's been so confused lately, and was so distraught. I should have called you. I know I should have. She hasn't been in all afternoon. I hope she hasn't gone and done something foolish."

"Mrs. Rollins, calm yourself. Take a deep breath. Now, listen to me," Rothman said, his voice quieter. "When Ms. McGill gets in, keep her here and call us. It's very important."

"Yes, detective, I certainly will."

Mrs. Rollins turned, and hurried back into the house. She entered the kitchen as Cardello was coming out of the pantry.

"The powder room's this way detective," she said, pointing toward the hall.

"Oh, I'm sorry," Cardello said. "I got confused."

Rothman was in the car when Cardello returned. She climbed in, a smile on her face. "Nice backup, Sam." Her hand came up for a high five. "Thanks."

"What was that all about?" Rothman asked her.

"Mrs. Rollins is from the old school. A woman like her would not leave the house with a hair out of place, much less her hat on crooked."

"You're implying?"

"She was in a real hurry to leave. I checked the kitchen. You can tell a lot about a woman by the way you find her kitchen. She left two tea cups sitting on the table. Brad only drinks coffee, so someone else was having tea with Rollins."

"The McGill girl's staying here," Rothman said. "The cups could have been left from early this morning."

"I don't think so. The kettle was still warm. Besides, Mrs. Rollins keeps an immaculate house. She would have washed the morning cups and put them away." Cardello looked at her watch. "We were here three hours ago. Ample time to clear the dishes. Either she was just entertaining someone else, which doesn't seem likely, or the girl hasn't been gone as long as she said. Something came up? Something so important that she didn't want to take the time to invite us in."

"She did seem to be in a hurry. No offer of her brownies today."

Cardello poked Rothman in the ribs. "Forget about your stomach. I also checked the phone on the desk beside the refrigerator. And the papers on the desk."

"Teri, you know what you tampered with might be evidence."

"Relax, I just shot a couple of pictures."

Chapter 43

Once back at the precinct, Cardello turned on her camera. "I'm not sure what this is," she said, handing the camera to Rothman. He studied the shot of a blue card, the size of a credit card, with three pictures circled in yellow. Before he could enlarge the photo to read the small print, Moses burst through the door, Paulie right behind him.

"That was fast," Rothman commented, looking at the boy's bandaged hands and ankles.

Paulie shrugged. "My sister-in-law works in the emergency room. Got this kid to the front of the line." Paulie took hold of Moses' shoulder, and led him to the chair near Rothman's desk. "You owe me one, man," he said as he left.

Rothman nodded.

Moses perched on the edge of the seat. He looked at the image on the camera in Rothman's hand. "Why you takin' pictures of that shit?"

"You know what that is?"

Moses leaned forward. "That there's a Spoof Card. It'll give you a fake ID, record a call, or change your voice. And you can have any name and number appear in the caller ID."

Cardello's glance met Rothman's.

Rothman turned his attention back to the boy. "We'll talk about this later. What do you know about Vickie Davis?"

"I saw how it went down. The whole thing."

"I'm sure you did." Lazaro suddenly filled the open doorway, blocking it.

"What is this? Am I under arrest or something?"

"No, Moses," Rothman said.

Lazaro turned toward Cardello. "Not yet," he said in a whisper loud enough for Moses to hear.

Moses jumped out of the chair. "What's that supposed to mean?"

"That's enough, Lazaro. Get the hell out of here." Rothman slammed the door in his face. Then he turned to Moses and said quietly, "Sit down."

Moses' distrust was evident as he eyed each detective, but slowly, he took his seat again.

"What was he talkin' about? I haven't done anything wrong. You find Ms. McGill. She'll vouch for me."

Cardello turned to Moses. "Moses, we found your basketball on Vickie Davis' fire escape."

"That's where I left it."

"So you admit you were there?"

"Sure I admit it. Like I said, I got nothin' to hide. Me and Vickie, we was friends. It's too late for her. But Ms. McGill, we got to find her."

"We're working on that. Now you talk to us, and be straight. Tell us about Vickie Davis. What did you see?"

"She was facing away from the door when it opened," Moses said. "Taking a bath. It all happened real quick. Vickie jumps up. The guy tells her to sit back down. He says something about an abortionist. About double-dipping. Charging for the abortion and then selling a baby."

"The guy? What did he look like?" Cardello, sitting on the edge of her desk, asked.

"I'm not exactly sure. He was wearing a long coat. Light brown. The collar was up, and he was wearing a hat. Lots of bushy brown hair. Tall. I never really saw his face."

"But you're certain it was a man?"

"Well, no. It could have been a woman, actually he did sound like a woman

Rothman referred to his notes. "The neighbor, Olivia, found her. Neighbors all confirmed that they heard one scream."

"That must have been Olivia who screamed when she came in and saw Vickie." Moses closed his eyes and shivered. "Jesus. When that guy pushed the hotplate into the tub, Vickie was dead before she could scream. I saw it."

"Moses, why do you think her door was unlocked?"

"She always left it unlocked. Window to the fire escape, too. She trusted people."

Rothman nodded.

Cardello said, "We're going to let you go now, Moses. Just make sure you don't disappear. I'm sure we'll have more questions for you."

Cardello was unwrapping her now-cold burger when the phone rang. The light indicated the line they shared. She put down the sandwich, and picked up the receiver.

"Thanks, Lazaro. Sam, the caller wants you."

"Put it on speaker, please, Teri."

"OK. Detective Rothman here." He stuffed some fries into his mouth. "How can I help you?"

"I can't get him out. He's stuck there. He's stuck." The loud, piercing voice would have been heard even without the speaker on. "You've got to help me. You've got to."

"Calm yourself down, ma'am, and tell me, who's stuck? Where?"

"My cat. My Snow Ball."

"Oh, is this Mrs. Kesselman?" Rothman turned toward Cardello. She covered her mouth to keep from laughing out loud.

"I'm sorry, Mrs. Kesselman, you were saying?"

"There's a new cat next door. My little Snow Ball was so upset with its mewing that she slipped into the apartment through the fire escape window. Now she won't come back out. There's no one home, and the super won't listen to me and open the door. If you don't come right now, I'm going to take matters into my own hands, and smash that window."

"Take it easy, Mrs. Kesselman. The other cat's probably just getting used to its new home. But I'll tell you what: I'll come by in a couple of hours and get your Snow Ball out. You wait for me. Don't do anything foolish, now."

Rothman rolled his eyes toward the ceiling, and clicked off the phone.

"Are you nuts? The woman's a loony toon," Cardello said.

"What the heck? It'll take just a few minutes." Rothman devoured the last of his Big Mac along with his fries. He threw his empty wrappings into the trash can.

Cardello flipped the pages on her note pad, and then flipped them again. "Sam, Moses described Vickie Davis' killer as wearing a long, light brown coat. And the super at McGill's place described the woman posing as McGill's aunt as wearing a long light colored coat." She pushed her chair back and stood up. "And Dirk, over at Rachel's just now, said the woman who gave him money to drive the VW also had a long coat. How do we connect them?"

Rothman began to reset an intricate maze of paper clips around his desk for the third time that day. "And the man McGill claims to have heard on the phone?"

"What if that was a woman using the Spoof Card Moses told us about? What if they were all women?"

Rothman had finished his maze and was now blowing slowly through a straw again, determined to direct a drop of water around the maze. "Or all one man?" He opened his mouth, the straw fell out and hit the paper clips. "I searched the upstairs rooms at Brad Dawson's when McGill called. Found costumes, makeup, and playbills in one of the wardrobe closets."

"So Dawson was probably involved in the theater," Cardello said. "Why else would he have those things lying around?"

"Exactly. He could be our man."

"But the aunt had a hump. She was stooped. The other two were described as being tall."

"There was something else in the wardrobe. It looked sort of like a fabric football, with a small harness at either end. It was about this long," Rothman held his hands up to his shoulders.

"And?"

Rothman looked through his drawers. He pulled out a small action figure he'd bought for Sammy, and tore it out of the package. He rolled a tissue into the shape of a tiny football and taped it to the doll's upper back. Then he draped another tissue over the shoulders, cape-like. He tilted the head forward.

"Let me guess. The Hunchback of Notre Dame."

"Or the woman claiming to be Mallory McGill's aunt."

Lazaro kicked open the door again.

"What the hell do you want now?" Rothman said, furious at his interruption.

"The reports on the gun just came in."

"Yeah?"

"The Glock's a pretty popular pistol, but there's no doubt. It's the same gun that killed the guy under the el. The striation from the barrel and the bullet in the stiff. A perfect match. We couldn't have done better."

"Yeah, so who do the fingerprints belong to?"

"Hold onto your hat." Lazaro was enjoying the center stage, and he wasn't about to be rushed. He lowered his voice to a whisper. "They belong to Bradford Dawson."

"Un-fuckin'-believable," Rothman said.

"Come on." Teri pulled her jacket off the hook.

Chapter 44

Mallory, in Keith's car, sped back to Thompson's, her hopes of finding her baby high.

The house, with its boarded-up windows, looked even more forlorn in the daylight, and now it looked menacing, too. Mallory was still trying to figure out why Brad would do something so awful as to take her baby, but she was sure of one thing: she was going to get her back. She opened the trunk, rummaged around, and pulled out a tire iron.

Slowly, she walked into the alley. The door stood slightly ajar.

Mallory climbed the three steps, and pushed the door open.

"Brad, I know you're here. Come out." Mallory's voice trembled, but she raised the tool above her head, and held her ground. Her demand was met with silence. She stood still and listened. Nothing.

She felt along the wall with her free hand until she found a light switch. Instantly, the room was awash in the harsh glow of a hanging fluorescent light, and she was staring at a table. White paper, fed from a roll at the head of the table, covered it. Stirrups dangled from the foot of the table. She touched the paper. Her fingers pulled it toward her, and she crunched it into a ball. Then she pulled more paper from the roll, and continued crunching it. At the sound of the crinkling paper, a cold chill coursed through her body. She saw herself strapped to that table. She heard her baby cry. The bar slid from her hand. "It was right here. This was the place."

Shaking, she turned away. She grabbed onto the edge of the sink to keep from falling. Her hand felt something wet and sticky. She looked at her palm: blood. She grabbed at a rag on the counter. Before she could wipe off the blood, she realized she was holding a tiny knitted cap—the kind hospitals put on newborns. And it was spotted with blood.

"No," she shrieked. "He wouldn't. He couldn't."

Chapter 45

Brad pulled into his driveway, his arms loaded with briefs. He took a deep breath, and walked up the path to his front door. His morning had been a busy one in court, and his head was still focused on a sticky custody case as he walked into the front hall and headed toward his office. But as soon as he heard Mrs. Rollins, he hesitated, his case forgotten.

"…you'd better be listening," she was saying. The rage in her voice ominous.

Brad heard her slam down the pantry phone, and run out the back door. He ran to the front door. As soon as Rollins pulled out of the driveway, he dashed to his car. He threw it into reverse, pressed his foot to the gas pedal, and shot out of the driveway. Cardello and Rothman were just pulling up. Cardello saw Dawson and slammed into his car, blocking his escape with her passenger door. She was out of the car in a flash. Rothman, shaken, slid across the seat, and was out a moment later.

"You freakin' morons. Look what you did. I've got to get to Mallory. She's in trouble," Brad said, jumping out of his car. "Move it. Move it," he banged on their windshield. "I've got to get to her."

"The only place you're going is to the precinct," Rothman said, drawing his gun. "You can tell us your story there."

"What are you talking about? If we don't get to her fast, it may be too late. Mrs. Rollins is going to kill her."

"Yeah, the housekeeper's going to kill her." Rothman rolled his eyes.

"She's crazy. She's after Mal. I heard her saying, 'McGill should have arrived by now. She better be dead before I get there.'"

Rothman and Cardello exchanged looks of disbelief. "You heard the *housekeeper* saying that?"

"Yes. She's out to get Mal."

"And why would that be?"

"I don't know."

"Of course you don't, because she has no motive. But you, on the other hand, have a very nice motive: your inheritance."

"That's ridiculous. That's more than ridiculous. I would have taken care of Mallory and the baby regardless."

Before Brad realized what had happened, Cardello cuffed his arms behind him. "You're being detained for questioning."

All Brad could do was watch as Rollins' car rounded the corner and moved out of sight.

"Mr. Dawson, do you own a gun?"

"Yes, a Glock 9mm but…"

"Do you keep it loaded?"

"No. But Mal… You're wasting your time with me. "

"Where is it?"

"I'm registered to carry it. I keep it in a locked box in my study. Got a permit a few years ago, after a wave of break-ins in the neighborhood."

The detectives, holding his cuffed arms, walked Brad back into the house.

"You'll find my keys there," he said nodding to the center desk drawer. "But hurry up. I told you Mallory's in trouble."

Rothman took a large key ring out of the drawer. "Which one is it?"

"I haven't gone into the box in a long time. I don't remember."

Rothman tried one key after another, while Cardello motioned Dawson toward a leather club chair near where he was standing.

As he was about to sit down, she noticed the tip of a file sticking out from under the seat cushion. With one eye on Dawson, she lifted the cushion and pulled out two manila folders. A cursory look at the name on the top folder made her look more closely. "Frank Assanato," she read.

At the mention of that name, Dawson looked up. "You found him? Where?"

"You know him," Rothman asked, pushing him back into the chair.

Cardello looked at the second one. Her eyes opened wide. "You're not going to believe this one, Sam." She dropped the folders on the desk. "Vickie Davis. Tell me, what did we do to get so lucky?" Then to Brad she said, "Mr. Dawson, I think you'll be needing a good lawyer."

With the very last key on Brad's key ring, Rothman opened the container. "It's empty," he said. "Why am I not surprised?"

"No. It can't be."

"Mr. Dawson, where's your gun?"

"Oh my God. Mrs. Rollins has the run of the place. She knows where I keep my keys. She knows all of my business and she's out to get Mal. She must have it."

"No doubt you're a smart attorney, and you know your rights, but I would like to read them to you, just so there's no misunderstanding while we talk.

"You have the right to remain silent. Anything you say can and will be used against you—"

"I know. I know," Brad said. "In a court of law. I have the right to have an attorney present during questioning. Yada, yada, yada. I understand these rights."

"Are you willing to talk to us without an attorney?"

"Yes."

Chapter 46

It was past four by the time Cardello and Rothman got back to the precinct with Dawson.

"You have no probable cause to hold me," Dawson said, once they'd brought him to the interview room. "You're wasting valuable time. Someone's going to die."

"Where were you last night?"

"I spend every Thursday night at the night court on Center Street. I serve as a legal aid attorney, pro bono."

"And you have witnesses who can verify that," Rothman said.

"Of course."

"Well, what about your dinner break? Did you leave the court house?"

"Nine to ten-fifteen. I ate at a Vietnamese restaurant around the corner on Baxter, with three other attorneys." He rattled off the names of the attorneys, two of whom Cardello was familiar with.

Cardello excused herself and made some calls. She returned a short time later. "Looks like your alibi is air-tight. You're free to go. Sorry we wasted your time. We'll arrange for someone to get you home."

"Damn," Rothman said, after a uniform had shown Dawson out. "I thought it would be just a matter of time until Dawson started talking. Figured we'd be able to wrap up the Frank Assanato case, and maybe the Vickie Davis murder would make some sense, too."

Lazaro barged in. "The report came in on the Gonzalez kid. No signs of a struggle. An overdose."

"Things are looking up a bit." Cardello took the report from him. She slid it into her file on Eduardo and wrote "Closed" across it.

As soon as Mrs. Rollins made the phone call she'd started to make earlier—before the detectives came by looking for McGill—she drove to the address she'd given Mallory. There was no sign of the girl or Thompson when she got there, but the blood on the counter made her nod.

She returned home. Dropping her purse on the hall console, she looked into the mirror above it, and tucked a loose strand of hair behind her ear. "One more loose end taken care of. Thompson will be the last," she said, and smiled.

Chapter 47

By the time she returned to her car, the tire iron and the baby cap clenched in her fist, Mallory's anguish had grown into a state of violent agitation. She drove around aimlessly, her tears blurring her vision.

"You stole my baby, Brad, and you killed her. How could you?" She raised the knitted baby cap to her lips.

Then, all at once, rage replaced her sorrow. "Brad Dawson, I'll get you, if it's the last thing I ever do. You and Mrs. Rollins, too. She knew. She told me to wait for you. Why? So you could kill me, too?" Her breath came in short bursts. She pulled over and stopped at a fire hydrant until her breathing became more regular. Then she drove carefully back to Bedford Avenue, and to Brad's. And this time she didn't park around the corner out of sight of the reporters.

It was late Friday afternoon. A few media people were still milling about when, blasting her horn, Mallory drove right into the driveway. The reporters scattered. She made a sharp left, drove across the manicured lawn, then over the border of flowers. She crashed into a huge ceramic planter next to the porch. The car stopped abruptly. Geraniums flew across the steps. Mallory's seatbelt cut into her, but held her tight. Mallory released the belt and grabbed the tire iron from the seat beside her. Once out of the car, she ran up to the porch. The reporters closed in on her. She swung around with the iron. They backed away. She opened the door and slammed it behind her. "I want some answers, and I want them now!"

Rothman gathered the desk full of paper clips to him. "We're back to square one."

"Maybe not. Maybe it was a woman who iced Vickie Davis, like Moses claimed. And maybe the woman posing as McGill's aunt really was a woman, too."

Rothman swept the clips into his center drawer. "That Spoof Card you found?"

"Maybe it wasn't Dawson disguising his voice. Maybe what McGill heard was a woman on the phone."

"Mrs. Rollins?"

"Could be."

"What if Rollins wanted her callers to think she was a man, or wanted them to think she was a particular man—say Brad Dawson?"

"The Spoof Card. Moses did say that you could set the card so that a different name and number would appear in your caller ID."

"Why would the housekeeper do something like that?"

"Rollins has been with Dawson since he was eight. She could be protecting him. She told me the brothers were rivals. Maybe there was some kind of inheritance thing."

"But if McGill wasn't married, she wouldn't stand to inherit."

"No. But her child would."

Lazaro threw open the door again. "The report on the cloth just came in. Seems the blood was McGill's and the bit of flesh on the sweater…" Lazaro paused.

"Well?"

"It was some kind of silicone used in prosthetics."

"The ear," Cardello said. "It was Mrs. Rollins who lied." She and Rothman grabbed their jackets and ran to the car.

Chapter 48

Mrs. Rollins hurried into the hall. "Child, you're back." She hesitated, then said, "You look flushed. Come sit down. I'll bring you a nice cup of tea, and you can tell me what happened."

Mallory caught the surprise in her voice. The old woman's sweetness no longer fooled her. "No. You tell me—everything you know." She grasped the tire iron with two hands.

Mrs. Rollins walked slowly to the console table. She reached for her purse, watching Mallory in the mirror over it as she did so. She pulled out a lace-edged handkerchief and, purse in hand, made her way to the living room, where she sat on the sofa.

Mallory hadn't taken her eyes off the housekeeper, nor had she eased her grip on the tire iron. "I'm waiting."

Mrs. Rollins sighed. "You were right. Brad is my son." There was a catch in her voice. She dabbed her eyes with her handkerchief. "I couldn't go against him."

"But my baby? Why did you…"

The housekeeper sighed. "I went to the old man for money. He was wealthy, but he refused. Said I'd ruined his son's life, and he wanted nothing to do with me."

"What does that have to do with my baby?"

Mrs. Rollins' face reddened. "It has everything to do with your baby," she screamed. "All I hear is your baby, your baby, your baby. Well, you're never getting her back. I was deprived of my baby, and you're going to be deprived of yours."

The housekeeper sat back on the couch. She ran her fingers along the piping on the edge of the brocade cushion. As quickly as she had raged out of control, she regained her composure. Her agitation gone, she picked a piece of lint off the arm rest, and studied it. "I showed him what ruin was."

"What are you talking about?"

"The old man. I knew he wouldn't leave his grandchildren out in the cold, should anything happen to their parents." She smiled. "So it did. They had a car accident the very next day."

"What are you saying?"

"You can't be that naive."

"No. You couldn't have…"

The old woman arched her left eyebrow. "Could have happened to anyone. They were driving on McDonald Avenue. Under the elevated tracks. A driver crossed the median. They swerved to avoid the car. Smashed right into the post."

"You were that driver?" A look of horror spread across Mallory's face.

She shrugged. "One has to do what one has to do. I came back to him later that same day. Said I'd heard about the accident on the news. He took me right in. I knew he would. He was totally distraught, and now he had two kids to deal with. Brad was just eight, and Keith was a baby. He said I could live with them—as the housekeeper. If I would agree to…"

"Agree to?"

The old woman walked over to the piano, her purse under her arm. She picked up the photograph of Brad as a baby.

"To never tell Brad that I was his mother."

"What about the baby you were carrying?"

"I had my pregnancy terminated."

"In the eighth month? But no ethical doctor…"

Mrs. Rollins laughed cynically. "Not every doctor is ethical." She wiped a fingerprint off the photograph. "It was easy to fool Brad. He was only two when I left. And in the six years, my appearance had changed drastically. I'd become gaunt, my beautiful blonde hair had become dry and brittle. It turned prematurely grey."

"I don't believe you. Brad's mother was Rita."

"When I came back, I changed my name. So there would be no chance of anyone connecting me to the past. I chose Ruth. From the Bible's Song of Ruth.

> *"Wherever you go, I will go;*
>> *wherever you live, there shall I live.*
> *Your people will be my people,*
>> *and your God shall be my God, too.*

"Can't you see the irony? Ruth of the good heart, obedient, faithful."

Before Mallory knew what was happening, Mrs. Rollins threw the framed photograph at her, reached into her open purse, and drew out a snub-nosed revolver, a .38 Special.

Mallory dropped the tire iron, and raised her hands.

"Damn you. I had it all worked out so carefully. The Grandfather. No one even questioned that. Everyone figured he died in his sleep."

"I can't believe that you would…" Mallory backed away. She tripped over the side table, breaking it as she landed on the floor. Stunned, she lay atop the splintered wood.

"He was lucky. I would have finished him off years ago," Rollins raged, "only Brad and Keith would have been assigned a court-appointed guardian, and the money would have disappeared."

Slowly, Mallory rose to a sitting position. She looked toward the tire iron she'd dropped. Mrs. Rollins saw her look, and kicked it away. The terrified girl inched away from Mrs. Rollins, until her back was against the wall, and her knees pulled up to her chin.

"I gave you a chance to leave. I offered you money. What more could I do? This is all your fault," Rollins' voice grew louder. "You chose to stay, you foolish girl."

"You'll never get away with this," Mallory said, with more bravado than she felt, as she stared at the gun in her face.

"Don't be so sure. Let's see…" Rollins looked away. "Oh, yes. 'Disturbed woman, temporarily insane, kills newborn child. Realizes what she's done and takes her own life.' It's a no-brainer."

Mallory's fingers inched toward the leg of the broken table lying beside her.

Rollins looked back at her,

Mrs. Rollins lifted her thumb toward the hammer of the gun. The front door opened, and she turned.

Mallory grabbed the table leg, and swung it at the housekeeper's arm. The gun flew across the parquet floor and into the hall as Brad, who'd pushed his way through the reporters, slammed the door shut.

Still on her hands and knees, Mallory lunged for the gun. The older woman leapt over her in a scramble to get to it first. Mallory grabbed Rollins' leg, and toppled her to the ground.

"What's going on here?" Brad grabbed Mallory's arm as she jumped up and sprinted toward the gun. She broke free of his hold and dived for it. Landing on her stomach, she grabbed the weapon and aimed it at Brad. "Over there," she ordered, breathing hard. "Join her." Unsteadily, she rose to her feet.

"Mallory, what are you doing? What's gotten into you?" Brad took a step toward her.

"I said over there," She stood taller, and motioned with the gun.

Brad backed away.

"Don't make like you didn't know all along. You were in this together. Mrs. Rollins told me. You were out to get my baby. Well, you won't get away with it. God help you both." Not taking her eyes off Brad and Rollins, Mallory stepped back, and squatted down to reach for the phone that had crashed to the floor with the table. The line was dead. She picked up the cord. It had come out of the wall.

"Mrs. Rollins, what is she talking about," Brad asked, keeping his arms in the air and his eyes on the gun in Mallory's hand.

"No need to be so formal with your mother," Mallory said.

"My *what*?"

"Brad, I was going to tell you. I *am* your mother."

"No. You can't be. I would have known."

"You were just two, a baby, you couldn't remember…"

"No. It's not possible. You can't be. My mother looked nothing like you."

"It was your grandfather. He threw me out of the house. Said I wasn't good enough for his son—he called me white trash."

Mallory gasped. "You told me you left… of your own accord."

"No. It wasn't like that. Brad, don't listen to her. She's crazy. Your grandfather threatened to disown you and your father if I didn't leave. I couldn't let that happen. Don't you see? I couldn't let him disinherit you. So I had to leave. Everything I did—it was all for you. Everything."

"I came right back when your father died. I couldn't leave you all alone."

Mallory's jaw dropped. She couldn't believe what she was hearing. Brad lunged for her. He grabbed her wrist with one hand, and the gun with the other.

Without releasing his hold on Mallory, he turned to the housekeeper. "Why didn't you tell me?"

"Your grandfather made me swear not to."

"And after he died?"

"Tell him how his grandfather died. Tell him," Mallory's voice grew louder as she struggled to free herself of Brad's strong grasp. "Go on. Tell him the truth."

"Brad, I don't know what she's talking about. You can't believe anything she says. She killed her baby. She wanted Keith's inheritance. All of it. I told you I found her marriage license. She was married to Keith. Without her baby, she stood to inherit whatever was Keith's."

Brad looked from Mallory to Mrs. Rollins, and back to Mallory again.

"Be careful. Please. Give me the gun, Brad. You've got to get it out of her reach."

"No, Brad. Don't do it," Mallory said, reaching for the gun. Brad stretched his arm up, out of her reach.

"Brad, I took care of you. You and Keith. All these years. I wiped your backsides, cleaned your noses. I did it all. You can trust me. You know you can." Slowly, Mrs. Rollins came toward him, her arms outstretched, her palms up. "I'll explain everything to you. But first, give me the gun, before Ms. McGill hurts you or herself."

"No, Brad. Don't," Mallory screamed. But Mrs. Rollins snatched it from his hand before he realized what was happening. She swung it back and forth, pointing it first at Brad, then at Mallory, then at Brad again.

"Mrs. Rollins, what are you doing? Put that gun down. Let's talk."

"No. It's too late for talk. You'll be sorry. Oh, Brad, don't you see. I had to protect you. I couldn't let your inheritance be taken from you. I bided my time until I could get the money for you, and then you spoiled it all."

"What are you talking about?"

"It was supposed to be just me and you, Brad. I should have shared in the wealth. This house should have been mine."

Rollins pointed the gun at Mallory's face and held it there. Mallory's eyes opened wide as she stared down the barrel. She felt as though she was seeing into a tunnel, or into the deep black hole of Mrs. Rollins' soul.

Brad put his arm around Mallory and pulled her close to him. "You're a sick, old woman."

Mrs. Rollins ignored Brad's words. Her face took on a look of fury. "But you had to be out that night, painting your stupid pictures," she said to Mallory. She turned the gun toward Brad. "And then you had to become her protector. You didn't care about me. When your brother died, you went to her. Not to me."

"Oh my God," Mallory covered her mouth with her hand. "That gas explosion was no accident. You killed Keith. And that look on your face when you saw me after… that wasn't relief. It was surprise. Surprise that I was still alive. I was supposed to be in that house."

"Yes. You and your precious baby were supposed to die with Keith. I would have killed you right after, if it wouldn't have made Keith's death look suspicious."

"But why? What did anyone ever do to you?" Brad asked, trying to win her over with the calmness in his voice.

"Don't you understand? All of this should have been mine," she said, waving the gun crazily around the room. "I had it all planned. You and me, the inheritance. They cheated me. I had to get rid of them. Well, at least I got rid of her child. At least I eliminated that."

Mallory slid to the floor, sobbing.

Brad couldn't contain his rage. "How could you," he said, advancing toward her.

"Don't, Brad." Mrs. Rollins cocked the hammer. The loud click echoed in the room. Brad stopped in his tracks.

"Favors for you, Brad. I called them in, your markers. Your pro bono cases."

"Those were indigent clients."

"They were scumbags. They owed you big time. I know. I did your billing."

"Owed big time. OBT." Mallory recited the letters. "Those cards. You marked them for yourself. Not for Brad. The house you sent me to?"

Mrs. Rollins nodded. "And that gas explosion. I did it for you, Brad. I did it all for you." Your father and his second wife. Your half-brother Keith, your grandfather. And the others that got in the way." Her voice was growing louder. "I was the one who sat up with you and cleaned up your puke when you were sick. I was the one who wiped your snotty nose when you cried. Can't you see? Everything I did was for you. For us. So that we could be a family again. Who else would have killed for you?" Her voice filled with venom. "Keith? He was plotting against me. And you betrayed me."

Then her voice became gentle. "But I forgive you, Brad. Once she's out of the way, it will be the two of us. The way it was supposed to be."

"You don't know what you're saying. It isn't too late. I can help you."

Rollins smiled. "Soon. Soon she'll be out of the way. It will be the two of us. Just the two of us." She aimed the gun at Mallory's chest.

"No," Brad shouted, diving on top of Mallory as Rollins pulled the trigger.

The bullet hit him just as the detectives kicked open the door.

Chapter 49

The call they'd been expecting came as Cardello and Rothman pulled into the hospital parking lot. Rothman put it on speaker. "Moses' description was good. We grabbed Thompson at JFK Airport. He had a ticket to Anchorage, one way. Had quite a bit of cash with him, too. Said he didn't believe in banks or credit cards. Get this: before we could say anything, he started talking. Said he wanted to plea bargain. Offered to turn state's evidence on Dantano and on the voice he thought was Dawson's."

"Mrs. Rollins. I still can't believe it. That nice old woman. I never would have suspected her," Cardello said, as she and Rothman entered the hospital elevator.

"She fooled me, too."

Upon hearing the detectives, Angela looked up from the nurses' station. "Your man was lucky. It was a clean wound. Straight through his back. The bullet missed the girl when he pushed her over. He'll be out in a few days." She nodded toward Brad's room across the hall. Moses was just coming out. "You're still all over the place," Rothman said, but this time he was laughing.

"Get used to seeing me around. I've decided on my career. I'm going to the police academy."

"We'll be glad to give you the highest recommendations," Cardello said.

"I'm figuring on that."

The shades were closed when they entered the hospital room. Brad was propped up, one arm in a sling. Mallory was standing beside his bed, holding a cup of water, the straw to Brad's lips.

Rothman cleared his throat. He pulled a photo out of his breast pocket. "Do you recognize this man, Ms. McGill?"

Mallory looked at the photo of Frank Assanato, the man found under the el. "That's him," she said excitedly, grabbing the photo. "That's the man who picked me up. I told you about his missing ear. Does he know anything about my baby?"

The detectives glanced at each other. They hadn't told Mallory about the baby formula they'd found on Assanato's shoes. And they hadn't yet been able to find an address for him. Rothman shook his head. "I'm sorry, Ms. McGill."

"What about the… uh, housekeeper," Dawson asked.

"The old girl was smooth. Real smooth," Cardello said. "She's still insisting that she heard a noise, and she didn't know it was you, Mr. Dawson, when she fired the gun. But rest assured, she won't be playing any more of her games for a long time to come."

Mallory turned to Brad. "I'm so sorry," she said. "All that time I blamed you."

"It doesn't matter any more."

Mallory sighed. "You're right. Nothing matters now."

Brad studied Mallory's face. With the palm of his good hand, he wiped the tears glistening under her eye. "I think it does."

Chapter 50

Mrs. Kesselman was waiting in the lobby when the detectives arrived. Cardello went right to the super for the key, as Rothman placated the distraught woman. It took just a few minutes to ride up to the sixth floor.

Rothman knocked on the door. A loud howl came from the interior of the apartment. He knocked more loudly. His pounding was met with a screeching meow, and then a thud. He unlocked the door. A white Siamese cat bolted out of the kitchen. It ran out of the apartment and skidded into the hall, then bolted up into Mrs. Kesselman's arms.

"My Snow Ball. My precious Snow Ball," she cooed to the cat. But there was more meowing coming from the apartment, muted meowing.

Rothman followed the sound. A chair beside the open oven door lay on its side, and on the floor beside it lay an overturned dresser drawer. The howling, grown more faint, was coming from beneath it.

Rothman lifted the drawer and gasped. He was looking not at a meowing cat, but at a crying newborn baby.

"Sam, is everything all right," Cardello called, coming up behind him. He scooped up the infant. Its loosely swaddled blanket fell away, and there on its right thigh was a purple strawberry-shaped mark.

"Everything is more than all right."

Acknowledgments

My sincere appreciation to my writing sisters for their unwavering support as they listened to draft after draft of this book. To my dear friends and family, I was fully aware of your restraint in not saying "enough already," as I talked endlessly about my book in progress. Thank you for humoring me. And thank you to Huey-Min Chuang, whose enthusiasm for my project created enthusiasm in others and drew them into it, and to Ronnie Rubin, for her close attention to detail within the book.

And the two people who most deserve my gratitude: Detective Barbara Stio, whose help has been invaluable. Without her wealth of knowledge, and her willingness to make herself available for my questions both day and night, this book might still be a work in progress. And Ian Randal Strock, my editor, my most severe critic, and my amazing son: I am forever in your debt.

Discussion Questions for Book Clubs

1. What made your group want to read this book? Was it all you expected it to be? Why? Do you think it would appeal to readers in general or only to readers of crime fiction?

2. Was the book clearly written? From whose perspective was the story told? Do you think that was a good choice on the part of the author?

3. What passage in the book resonated with you most? What did it reveal about specific characters or particular aspects of the story?

4. Did the novel hold your interest throughout the story, or were there parts you felt might have been shortened, lengthened, or eliminated?

5. How far along were you in the book before you began to put the pieces together? Were you able to guess the villain's identity before it was revealed? If so, how?

6. How did setting this story in the seedier part of Coney Island make you feel? Was it realistic?

7. What red herrings did the writer use to throw you off track?

8. What part of the story worked best: the dialog, the setting, the characterizations? How realistic and/or believable was: the dialog, the settings, the characterizations? Which character's dialog did you find most effective?

9. Did the plot move along smoothly? Were the motivations of the characters believable, or did you feel that the characters' motivations were forced to move the story along?

10. Who were your favorite characters and why?

11. Did you feel as though you knew each of the characters well? Why?

12. The author has written a women's issues book and a how-to/self-help book in addition to this mystery. How do you feel about a writer writing in more than one genre?

CPSIA information can be obtained at www.ICGtesting.com
Printed in the USA
BVOW05s1745190815

413968BV00001B/7/P